IT WAS JUST A LITTLE

I don't know if I'll ever b... happened next. I guess I s... not exactly crazy. Anyway, ... down and kissed him on th... he did? He kissed me back on the cheek. Just like that!

I was in such a daze I hardly remember saying good-bye. Next thing I knew, I was out on the street walking home, except I didn't feel like I was walking at all. It was more like floating. The imprint of his lips still burned on my cheek. I touched my face. There was nothing there. Still, I knew it would be a long time before I washed that spot. I couldn't believe how wonderful it felt. Robert Mitchell had kissed me.

LONG TIME BETWEEN KISSES

"Wit and humor, and finely drawn characters...work together to flesh out this bittersweet identity crisis and first love."

—*Voice of Youth Advocates*

"Quite deftly handled.... Billie is an engaging character, purple hair and all."

—*University of Chicago Press*

"Scoppettone's characters—even the minor ones— are carefully drawn. She knows them well and stays with them, so that the timing and dialogue are true."

—*School Library Journal*

"A streetwise novel of New York City presents a hard-boiled—but fundamentally softhearted—heroine.... The easygoing, sociable Soho neighborhood is depicted realistically, the book generates a warm and friendly feeling."

—*The Horn Book*

Long Time Between Kisses

Sandra Scoppettone

BANTAM BOOKS
TORONTO • NEW YORK • LONDON • SYDNEY • AUCKLAND

RL5, IL age 12 and up

LONG TIME BETWEEN KISSES

*A Bantam Book / published by arrangement with
Harper & Row, Publishers, Inc.*

PRINTING HISTORY
*Harper & Row edition published April 1982
Bantam edition / November 1984*

*Starfire and accompanying logo of a stylized star are trademarks
of Bantam Books, Inc.*

*Bantam Books are published by Bantam Books, Inc. Its trade-
mark, consisting of the words "Bantam Books" and the por-
trayal of a rooster, is Registered in U.S. Patent and Trademark
Office and in other countries. Marca Registrada. Bantam
Books, Inc., 666 Fifth Avenue, New York, New York 10103.*

One

Early this morning I cut off all my hair. Real short. Like to about an inch long all over. Tomorrow I'm going to dye it purple.

Why?

Why not? I think it looks neat. And purple hair is really cool. At least it is where I live. Maybe if we still lived where we used to, in the suburbs, it wouldn't be so cool, but we moved here to SoHo in New York City when I was eight. Now I'm almost seventeen. Well, sixteen and five months. So who's counting? SoHo, which means South of Houston Street (pronounced like house, not like the one in Texas), is a really neat place to live. Way back in the Sixties people started buying these buildings that had factory spaces in them and began turning them into places to live called lofts. They're like real big apartments. For instance, our loft is three thousand square feet. If you can't picture that, believe me, it's big. The Mother says it's the only way to live in New York City and I guess she's right. Of course it's just the two of us now in all that space. The Father moved out about a year ago.

But don't feel sorry for me or anything. I

don't. And I don't feel like I come from a broken home or any dumb thing like that. There's nothing broken about it. I mean, these things happen. The Mother and The Father just couldn't swing it anymore. No big deal.

The Father lives three blocks away in a regular apartment. Not a loft. He lives with Her. The Organic Woman. Feh!

Anyway, SoHo's this terrific place to live. Lots of artists and writers and musicians and people like that live here. And not phonies either. These people really do their work—they don't just talk about it. SoHo is bordered by Greenwich Village, an area called NoHo (you probably can figure out what that stands for), Little Italy, the Bowery, the Lower East Side and another area called TriBeCa. And from my loft Chinatown is a fifteen-minute walk. So you can see it's sort of international around here, which is very broadening.

The only trouble with SoHo is that in the last few years it's become very chic. The place is loaded with Art Galleries and real expensive restaurants and these way-out boutiques. So a lot of people from out of town and uptown come down here to gawk and spend a lot of money and think that *they're* chic. The thing of it is that *we* don't think *we're* chic at all. I mean, that's not the point. When most of us moved here it was 'cause it was cheap and we could have a lot of space to do our work.

For example: The Mother, when we moved here, was a sculptor. She made these huge wooden things. And I mean huge. I also mean *things*. Year after year she chopped and hacked away at these creations that looked like something from Mars and called them stuff like: LIFE. BIRTH. DEATH. WOMAN. It was plain embarrassing. I don't mean to give the impression that The Mother was a phony artist or anything. She worked very hard and was real serious about it. She just stunk.

But here's the really neat thing about her. One day she called me and The Father into her studio and sat us down and pointed to her latest piece called: THE COUPLE and said, "Tell me the truth, what do you see?"

What I saw was this giant piece of wood with a lot of sharp corners sticking out. So what do I know about art? I mean who am I to say? But she asked. So I said, "I see this piece of wood with some sharp corners and jagged edges."

"Right," she said. "And you, Ted?"

The Father ran a hand through his long black hair, scratched, and said, "I see the same as Billie."

"Right."

Then there was this long silence while The Mother stared at THE COUPLE. "You want to know something," she goes, "that's what I see, too. I really stink."

Well, for a few seconds both me and The Father started hemming and hawing 'cause who wants to say that your mother and your wife is a lousy artist. You know how it is. You can go along for years thinking something about a person, and then when they come to it themselves you try to tell them it isn't true. Why is the truth so scary? Anyway, while the two of us are going through this big act, The Mother is standing there in all of her five-foot-two splendor, head cocked to one side, looking at us like we're nuts. Finally she goes, "Hey, hold it, gang." She always called us gang. I think it's 'cause she wanted to have a gang of kids and all she came up with was me. So she goes "hold it" and we stop the rap and she says, "I'm not kidding around. I didn't say I stink so that you would go into a whole number about how good I am. I said it because I believe it and I know you do too. And it's okay. I wouldn't have been ready for it if you'd told me that last year or last month or maybe even yesterday. Today I'm ready. I stink. I'm no sculptor."

"Don't you feel bad?" I asked.

She sat down in front of THE COUPLE, crossed her legs, and put her chin in her palm. "I suppose I would if that was that. But it isn't. It came to me yesterday. I really like working with wood but I'm just no sculptor. So I asked myself, what else can I do and I thought, I could be a carpenter."

The Father laughed. "You're not serious?"

"Very," she answered, balling her small hands into fists.

Well, this was typical of them. He never had much confidence in her or gave her much support, especially when it came to things she wanted to do that weren't things women usually do. I hate to say it but The Father was, and is, a bit of an MCP. Male Chauvinist Pig. I hope he'll get better but living with The Organic Woman I don't see how he can.

"What kind of a carpenter?" I asked.

"Well, like cabinets and bookcases and maybe nice tables and pretty boxes and rooms and lofts and houses." Her brown eyes kept getting bigger and wider.

This just doubled The Father over into huge guffaws. It made me hate him. I think it's uncool to laugh at anybody's dream no matter what. And The Mother was not an innocent when it came to that either. Not by a long shot.

You see, his dream is to be a famous musician. He plays the clarinet, and he does okay but he's no household word, like they say. He's into jazz and plays with a combo and gets gigs all the time. Gigs are jobs. His group is called Ted James (that's him) and The Commanders. I think that's a really boring name and I told him so. I think he'd get a lot better gigs if he called his group The Freakouts or The Fatal Flaw or Killers Kiss or something neat like that. He says I don't understand his music or his age. Maybe so. Anyway, The Mother doesn't understand it either. She says she hates jazz. Why did they ever get married? So she's hardly been supportive of him either, and when he used to talk about being number one she'd say things like "lots of luck" or "I'll believe it when I see it." Big help. Of course, The Father did give her some reason to feel that way. Still, I don't think it was too cool to *say* it. You see, he's a pothead and that drove her crazy. She said he wasn't really there and he lived in fantasy and I guess she was right. But more about that later.

Here's the P.S. to The Mother wanting to be a carpenter. She is one. And a real good one. She was even featured in *New York* magazine's Best Bets section. And other people have done articles about her, like *Reader's Digest* and *The New York Times* and *Ms.* magazine. She's come to be known as Arley Carpenter even though her name is really Arley James. I'm very proud of her. She taught herself from books, and she apprenticed with this guy Ben and he taught her stuff, and now she's on her own and she does just what she wanted to do. Sometimes she makes pretty things like tables and cabinets and sometimes she builds whole lofts. Rooms and bathrooms and kitchens. She hasn't built a house yet. But building the inside of a loft is almost the same. Sometimes when I go see one of these places she's built I almost can't believe it. It really knocks me out.

And I guess I'm jealous, too. You see, I don't have any talent. Don't think I haven't tried to develop one. I've tried writing, painting, acting, singing, playing the guitar, and photography. And guess what? Nada. Zero. Zip. You can't imagine what it's like to want to be creative and there's just nothing there. Well, maybe you can imagine. It's depressing. It makes me feel like a nobody. A nothing. The Mother says you're not what you do but that's easy for her to say. I hate not doing something special. It's boring. I hate to be bored or boring. I especially hate to be boring. There's nothing worse.

So I thought it would be interesting to cut my hair real short and dye it purple. There's nothing boring about that. This afternoon I went into Arley's workshop and sat on a stool and watched her making this truly beautiful table out of teak. She had her back to me but she knew I was there 'cause I said hello when I came in.

"So what's new?" she asked.

"Nothing."

"What've you been up to?"

It was the first day of summer vacation. "This and that."

"Terrific. What this and what that?" She started hand sanding.

"Ah, you know."

"If I knew, Billie, I wouldn't ask."

"Yeah, I guess."

"Hey, you didn't come in here for your health, did you?

"Nope."

Then there was this quiet between us, like it was kind of ominous, I guess, and she stopped sanding, stood up, and real slow like turned around to look at me.

I wish I'd had a camera. You know what they say about a picture being worth a thousand words? Arley Carpenter was blown away. Her eyes got big as poker chips and her mouth fell open and then she goes, "Billie, your hair!"

I was grinning back at her and feeling tingly inside. You know how it is when you plan something and it happens exactly the way you thought? Especially when it's with The Mother or The Father. It's like ringing a bell, winning a prize. Yahoo!

Then she goes, "Why?"

"Why what?"

"Don't be provocative. Why'd you cut your gorgeous hair like that? You look awful."

"Thanks."

"Well, you know you do."

Actually, I didn't. "I like it."

"You look like a creep. You looked so pretty with your long brown hair."

"Maybe I don't want to look pretty."

"Well, why not? Is there something wrong with looking nice?"

"You said pretty."

"All right, is there something wrong with looking pretty?"

"Yes. It's a feminist issue."

"Oh, spare me," she said. "Being yourself is a feminist issue."

"Well, this is me."

"I'm sorry to hear that."

"I'm leaving," I said.

"Good. I don't want to look at you anymore." She turned her back as I got down off the stool. Before I left the workshop I stuck my tongue out at her. I know it was childish, but it made me feel good.

The thing is I don't understand why I felt bad when she said those things. It was *exactly* what I knew she'd say. Every last word. So why was I depressed?

Here I was lying on my bed and feeling like a nerd. I liked my hair short. I didn't want to be a sex object looking all sweet and pretty and sexy. Right? Wrong. Let's face it, I didn't cut my gorgeous long brown hair that I'd grown for years and years for that reason, and I don't know why I made The Mother think that that's why I did it. So why did I do it? I don't know, and maybe that's why I felt like this cold wet gray lump of clay was just lying in my gut.

The thing of it is I got up this morning, put on my glasses, looked in the mirror, and said: "Billie, this is the first day of summer vacation and you're nowhere and nobody. Yes, you have this boyfriend who says he loves you but so what? Dino Farelli is real cool and one of the

Bonus Boys and you couldn't have a better boyfriend than that. Maybe having a boyfriend isn't everything it's cracked up to be."

And then I picked up the scissors and I cut off my hair. Chop, chop, chop. When it was done I felt high.

And then I didn't. Because I let The Mother bring me down. So what should I do? Should I lie there and sulk? Or should I go out and look for some more people to bring me down? Was that a choice? I was getting real negative and I didn't like it. I listed my options.

Going to see The Father. Out.

Lying there like a noodle. Out.

Meeting Dino. Out. (He was working.)

Then it came to me like out of the heavens. Maybe my best friend Elissa was back from visiting her Aunt Ruthie in the Bronx and was having a cappuccino at our hangout Vinnie's, which was a kind of luncheonette two blocks away. I decided to go.

While I was waiting for the elevator, I thought about wearing my blue baseball cap so I wouldn't just shock everybody. But then I thought, who cares what they think? It's my hair and I like it.

The elevator opened and Roger, an upstairs neighbor, was on it and he goes, "Billie, what'd you do to your hair?"

What a dumb question. It was perfectly clear what I'd done. I hate when people ask you these dumb questions but you're supposed to be polite and answer just like it wasn't dumb.

"I cut it," I said.

"Well, that's obvious," he said.

If that wasn't a real face smacker, I don't know what was. But I smiled sweetly.

"You look like hell," he said.

The door of the elevator opened and Roger marched out in front of me, calling back over his shoulder: "You'd better get a wig."

He was out the front door before I could tell him what a wimp he was.

As I walked down Prince Street toward Vinnie's, I began to think maybe dying my hair purple wasn't the best idea I'd had in a while. On the other hand, I'd gone this far so why not?

Sometimes you have to just go all out, you know? You've got to take risks in life and not give a hoot in hell what anybody else thinks. Be yourself. Be your own person. Yeah.

"Hello, Pinhead," a guy said, almost knocking me in the gutter.

I crossed the street to Vinnie's wondering if I had enough in my savings account for a wig.

Two

I thought Vinnie would never stop laughing. Watching him, I had mixed emotions. Half of me wanted to belt him one, the other half thought about getting him an oxygen tank as he sputtered and coughed and turned red in the face.

The place was crowded with regulars, kids, housewives, some of the "boys." When Vinnie started laughing, everything stopped. Even the pinball machine, which always had action, was left unattended. The only sounds in Vinnie's Luncheonette were the ever-present voices from the old black-and-white television and this horrendous laughing from Mr. Big V. At least they were all looking at him instead of me. Well, for a bit. Then he raised his arm and pointed at me. A million eyes shifted. I thought I'd die. I could've run out, I suppose, but I didn't. Instead I said, "Cappuccino for the house." Lucky for me nobody could hear over Vinnie's laughing 'cause I only had two bucks with me.

I sat down at an empty table and waited for the whole thing to end. Finally Vinnie pulled himself together and came over to me. He wiped his eyes with the end of his stained apron.

"Hey, Billie, whatcha do to yer hair?"

Here we go again, I thought. "I had a permanent."

"Oh, yeah? Well, they didn't cook it long enough or somethin' 'cause it still looks straight. Looks like you chopped it off yourself."

Brilliant.

Vinnie reached out and touched my crew-cut ends. "Who gave you this permanent, huh? You want I should talk to him?"

"No thanks," I said. "I was only kidding, Vinnie. No permanent. I cut it myself like you thought. So can we forget it now?"

"Kids." He shook his head and made a clucking sound. "Whatayawant?"

"Cappuccino." I watched him walk away still shaking his head. The Mother thinks Vinnie is very handsome. She says he has a patrician nose. I looked that up. It means noble or aristocratic. Beats me. Anyway, I guess he is handsome for an older man and if you like that dark type. Me, I go for blonds. Maybe that's why Dino doesn't do it for me completely. He's dark, too. The Mother also thinks he's handsome.

"One cap," Vinnie said, putting the cup in front of me. In case you don't know, cap—short for cappuccino—is espresso coffee and steamed milk with cinnamon on top. Vinnie eyeballed me again and broke into a big grin. I ignored him and stirred my cappuccino.

I was glad to see the crowd in Vinnie's was back to normal, everybody minding their own business. Sort of. The door opened and Captain Natoli and his little dog Pinocchio came in. We called him Captain 'cause he always wore a blue officer's cap. Captain Natoli was the oldest man I'd ever met. And the smallest. Nobody knew exactly how old he was, but everyone agreed he was in his nineties. He was smaller than The Mother by at least two inches so he couldn't have been more than five feet.

"Hello, young girl," he said to me, touching the brim of his hat with two fingers. He always called me that. In fact, when he saw me with The Mother he'd say, "Hello, young girls." I guess almost everyone looked young to him.

"Hello, Captain Natoli, how are you today?" I reached out to pet Pinocchio and he licked my hand from his toothless mouth. Pinocchio, in dog years, was about as old as the Captain.

"Justa fine, young girl. Howa you?"

"Good."

"Nicea girl."

When the Captain moved on to the next table I realized he hadn't noticed my hair. At least he hadn't made any cracks about it. No wonder I'd always liked him. Vinnie often complained about him because he spent a lot of time in the place talking, talking, talking about the past. Sometimes he drove Vinnie nuts. And yet he was kind to him, often giving him free lunches.

The door opened again. It was Elissa. Right away I felt sunnier. Elissa almost always had that effect on me. As far as I'm concerned everybody needs a best friend. Somebody to share things with. Somebody who never puts you down. Somebody you can trust. The Father says you can't trust anyone. The Mother says that's his marijuana paranoia talking. I think she's right.

"Hiya, pal," Elissa said sitting down opposite me. We called each other pal 'cause we thought it was funny. Once for a present Elissa gave me this old Valentine with a poem on it called "Pal o' My Heart." It was a hoot.

Elissa gave me the onceover, her brown eyes going to work on my hair. While she looked she ran her hands through her own black curls. Then she goes, "So, not bad. Who, when, why?"

"I did it myself. This morning. I don't know why."

"Yeah, that's how it goes. Your mother see it?"

I told her what happened.

"To be expected. What do they know? I like it."

"Really?"

"Have I ever lied to you?"

I shook my head. It was true. Elissa never lied to me.

"So I'm not gonna start now," she said. "It's not as nice as it was, but it's not bad and everybody needs a change now and then."

"I was thinking of dying it purple."

"What shade?"

"I hadn't thought."

"Very important. Vinnie," she called, "one cappuccino, please. The shade is everything."

"You really think I should do it?"

"If you want. Why not?" She smiled, showing one long dimple. "It's *your* hair. You gotta right to do what you want with it, you know."

"Yeah. Well, maybe lavender."

She shook her head. "Too light for your skin coloring. I think purple purple."

"Neat. I'll do it tomorrow."

"Terrif."

Vinnie put her cappuccino on the table. "So how do you like Chicken Head?"

"And who might that be?" asked Elissa.

"Are you kiddin'?" He smiled big and his two eyeteeth started looking very long all of a sudden.

When he was gone Elissa goes, "He's not the Sassoon of SoHo, you know."

I laughed and right away started feeling better. "So how was Aunt Ruthie?"

"Aunt Ruthie's always great," she said, "and a lot better than Sylvia, but who wouldn't be?"

Sylvia was Elissa's mother, who was kind of crazy. She was always going in and out of mental hospitals. Sometimes she was perfectly all right and would sit around and talk to us sort of regular like, but then other times she'd do peculiar things. Like one night I was over at the Rosenbergs' for dinner and Elissa's father, Herman, goes, "Sylvia, can't you ever get the dinner on the table on time?"

Sylvia eyeballs him, goes to the kitchen, picks up this pot of stew, carries it to the table, and says, "You want the dinner on the table, Herman? Your wish is my command." And then she turns the pot upside down and pours the stew all over the table, throws the pot on the floor, and goes to her room.

Things like that.

The Mother says Elissa comes from a real unstable environment. Don't get me wrong, Arley Carpenter loves Elissa. But then, everybody does. Except maybe Andy, who's Elissa's twin brother. But that's another story.

"She says hello to you, by the way. Aunt Ruthie, that is."

"Hello back." I liked Aunt Ruthie a lot. She didn't have any kids of her own, so she took us places, like to movies, theater, museums, and stuff, and she talked to us like we were grown-ups.

"Anyway, never mind Aunt Ruthie for now. I want to talk to you about Dino and Mickey."

Mickey was Elissa's boyfriend and the other Bonus Boy. "What about them?"

"They're up to something."

"Like what?"

Elissa said, "Last night I bumped into them and started rapping. They were acting all weird." She lit a cigarette. Elissa smoked like a chimney. It was the only thing I didn't like about her 'cause I don't approve of smoking.

"Don't," she goes.

"Don't what?"

"Don't give me that look because I'm lighting up. Keep your narrow judgments to yourself."

"It's no narrow judgment. It's 'cause I love you and I don't want you dying of the Big C."

"Don't."

"But Eliss . . ."

"Just don't. You wanna hear about the guys or not?"

"Yeah." I'd tried a million times, a million ways, to discourage her from smoking but nothing worked. "Go ahead," I said.

She blew a big stream of smoke out of the corner of her mouth. "So, anyway, they were acting real strange, like they had a secret or

something. I said, did they want to go over to
The Owl and play some pinball and they go,
no, they'll see me later. I say, where you going,
they go, got a business appointment. And they
split." She shrugged her shoulders and sipped
her cappuccino.

"You think they're dealing again?"

"I don't know. Maybe, but I don't think that's
what it was."

I sure hoped not. The Bonus Boys used to sell
pot. And the reason they got that name was
'cause they always gave a little extra. But when
Elissa and I got involved with them we made
them give it up. Still, the name stuck and now
they did odd jobs and always gave a little extra
there, too. "How come you don't think it was
that?"

"They were too weird. If they're dealing again
I think they'd try to cover better, don't you? I
mean they know if they deal again they lose
us." She grinned like we were a couple of
prizes worth not losing.

"Did you ever think that might be just the
point?"

The grin disappeared like chalk from a blackboard. See, Elissa really was in love with Mickey,
and if he decided to dump her she always said
it would be the end of her life. Somehow I
doubted it. Not that I doubted her love for him
but I instinctively believed her life would go on.
Somehow. Some way. With my help and support, of course. Besides, she had a lot to do
with her life. Elissa was a neat singer and
someday she was going to be as famous as Joan
Baez. Anyway, I know a lot of people don't
believe you can really be in love at our age, and

though I don't believe I've ever been in love (unless you count the way I felt about Mrs. Cooley, my fourth-grade teacher...but then I guess maybe that would fall in the crush category), I believe with all my heart and soul that Elissa Rosenberg was truly and deeply and passionately in love with Mickey Zellan.

Elissa was suddenly white as paper and her cheeks were sunken in like all her teeth had been pulled. "Billie, you think Mickey's got somebody else?"

"Nah," I said. And I didn't.

"We gotta find out what they're up to." The color was slowly coming back into her cheeks.

"Why didn't you follow them?" A lot a times I followed people on the street like I was Billie On The Case, and I'd taught Elissa how to do it and not get caught.

"I thought about it and I watched them go. They kept turning around looking back, watching me. There was no way."

"Sounds like they're up to something."

"Really," she goes.

Then we were interrupted by Captain Natoli.

"Hello, young girls." He tipped his hat, then stroked Pinocchio's head while he held him with his other arm. "On Christmas day alla da family would come, bringin' presents anda the chillern, alla da lil kids. Hello, Papa, they'da say, Merry Christmas." He smiled happily and stroked the white hairs on the dog's brown head.

"That's nice, Captain Natoli," Elissa said.

I wondered what triggered memories of Christmas on June 25th when it was eighty degrees out. "Very nice," I added.

"Good-bye, young girls," he said and was off, slowly inching his way toward the door. It was odd to know that all his children were dead. But he had lots of grandchildren and great-grandchildren and even some great-great-grandchildren. Vinnie said none of them ever visited though. Sometimes people could be rotten. Still, he seemed happy with his dog and his memories. A lot more than some people had. A lot less, too.

"What are we going to do?" Elissa asked.

"About what?"

"The boys."

"Oh, yeah. Well, surveillance is in order, I guess." I snapped my fingers. Idea! "Hey, with my new look they might not recognize me. I'll put on dark glasses and I'll be able to follow them easy."

"Yeah," Elissa goes enthusiastically. "You got any clothes that Dino and Mickey won't recognize?"

"If I just wear a work shirt and jeans it'll be all right."

"Yeah. Cool."

So me and Elissa finished our cappuccinos and planned to meet after dinner in the park. That's Washington Square Park. Dino and Mickey always met there at seven-thirty, so we knew we could see them there and then follow them. It was a good plan and we both felt confident that the so-called mystery would be revealed that night. I could hardly wait.

Three

"Where are you going?" from The Mother.

We'd finished dinner and I was on my way to meet Elissa in the park. "Out," I said.

"I'd like you to stay home tonight, Billie."

Wait a sec, I thought. What's going on here? The dinner was eaten, the dishes were stacked in the washer, and I'd even taken the vitamins that Arley Carpenter was always shoving at me. I tried to act calm. No sense giving her a feeling of urgency. Sometimes if they knew how much you wanted to do something, it made them all the more set on whatever it was they had in mind for you. So I go, "Oh, yeah? How come?" Casual like.

The Mother sat on one of the high counter stools and pulled at her rose-colored T-shirt, which was sticking to her from the humidity. "There's someone I'd like you to meet."

This could only mean one thing, but I acted dumb. "Yeah, who?"

"A friend." She picked at her lower lip, which she always did when she was nervous or insecure.

"What friend?"

She cleared her throat, plucked at the shirt, twisted the lip. The woman was a mess. "His name is Tom Chase."

You know, she really drove me nuts. Tom Chase. Ted James. Why did she have to pick these noodles? Something a little more ethnic would have suited me better. Some glamor. Some pizzazz. Some something. James. Chase. Feh! "Well," I said, reaching for a no-sweat tone, "I'd like to meet him but I have an important appointment tonight."

"You always have an important appointment, Billie. This is important to *me*."

"Yeah? What's the big deal? I can meet a friend of yours any old time. What's so important about meeting some wimpy friend of yours?" Now don't get me wrong, I'm no dummy. I knew this was no ordinary friend 'cause The Mother was more casual about friends. She had had a few dates since The Father had moved out but I hadn't met any of them. So one plus one meant two, or this was somebody sort of special. Besides my brilliant addition, I could tell by the glint in her eyes and the way her hands were wrestling with each other like two small opponents. Tom Chase was a Boyfriend! So why was I playing games with The Mother? Because I wanted it straight. If she couldn't come right out and say I'd like you to meet a new man I'm seeing, or the equivalent, then why should I stay home from my very important appointment? So call me Hard-Hearted Hannah, I don't care.

"He's not a wimpy friend," she said softly.

"What is he?" What more of an opening could I give?

She stood up, went to the refrigerator, got out some apple juice, went to the cabinet, and got a glass. Pouring the juice, her back to me, she goes, "Never mind, forget it."

Did I feel like a rat? Yes. I thought about going up behind her and putting my arms around her, but I couldn't remember the last time I'd done anything like that so I scratched the idea. Physical contact was not where it was at with me and The Mother. Like ice cream in August my rathood melted. If she couldn't be honest with me then she didn't deserve my presence. So long, kiddo!

It was still hot when I hit the street. Well, not exactly hot, more wet, like I'd walked into a sauna. I turned at Prince and West Broadway and headed up toward the park. I was about five minutes late, but Dino and Mickey usually hung around for a while before going anywhere so I figured it'd be okay.

A lot of people were out on the streets. And a lot of nuts. Warm weather always brought them out, like wild flowers. I guess in the winter they had themselves put in jail or hospitals or they just huddled in doorways, but the minute it turned warm, there they were, mumbling or shouting to hordes of invisible people (some friends, some enemies), and scaring the pants off the tourists. But they didn't scare me. I felt sorry for them and I knew they were in their own kind of pain, and I also knew there was nothing I could do for them. And then there were the creeps.

Them I wasn't too hot for. They were the ones who said dirty things, and made ugly sounds at you, the ones I wanted to belt in the chops but knew the best, the safest thing to do was to give them a wide berth. *Ignore* was the catchword for them.

I crossed West Fourth to the park. The minute I entered, the usual chant began.

"Smoke, smoke, smoke."

"Colombian gold. Good dust."

"Pure coke."

"Ups, downs, anything you want. Best smoke in town."

You confused? You don't know what that is? These were the park salespeople. They came in both sexes, all ages, and many colors. What they were selling was drugs. I could've gotten anything I wanted but I didn't want a thing. Just because it's available doesn't mean you gotta do it. I kept shaking my head no as I walked past them and headed up the path toward University Place where I was to meet The Pal!

She was waiting behind the tree we'd agreed on.

"Hurry," she said, looking wild-eyed and frantic.

"How come you recognized me?" I asked, touching my dark glasses.

"Very funny. They're just leaving the park and they've been looking over their shoulders and stuff, real suspicious like. I think they're spies."

"Spies? Spies for what?"

"I don't know. C'mon, let's follow them."

I said, "You can't come—they'll recognize you."

"No, they won't." She whipped out a red baseball cap from her back pocket, pulled it down over her curly hair, and from another pocket took something else. She turned her back to me for a second, then faced me, smiling.

What she had on was a pair of those fake glasses with a big nose and a mustache. It was all I could do to keep from rolling on the ground. Even when Elissa wore normal sunglasses she looked peculiar. And hats of any kind were a disaster on her. But this!

"What's wrong?" she asked, seeing the look on my mug. I was on the verge of uncontrollable and prolonged laughter.

"You look like something out of a Woody Allen movie," I said. "They'll spot you in a sec. Take that off."

"They won't and I won't. Let's go, we're wasting time."

So, it was Billie And Elissa On The Case!

The guys were walking fast and me and Elissa had everything we could do to keep up with them. Not that boys necessarily walk faster than girls do or anything like that, but we've both got short legs. Still, we kept them in sight. Elissa had been right. They kept looking over their shoulders and acting generally suspicious. It was either some big drug sale they were involved in or they *were* spies. What else could it be?

When we got to Sixth Avenue and Eighth Street it was getting a little harder to hide, and now people were starting to eyeball us. All the way across Eighth nobody had even blinked an eye. That tells you what Eighth Street's like. Freak Heaven!

The guys crossed Sixth and headed up Greenwich Avenue. We were far enough behind and there were enough people on the street and it was getting dark, so they still didn't pick up on us.

"They're spies, I know they are, the bums," Elissa said. "They'd sell out their country in a minute."

"Stop," I said. "We don't know anything yet."

"Traitors," she spat out.

"Cool it."

Ahead of us the boys took a left on Charles Street. We waited at the corner until we figured they were far enough down the block so we could turn undetected.

A man with glasses, a mustache, and a big nose pointed at Elissa and cracked up as he passed us.

"I wonder if we're related?" Elissa asked.

At Seventh Avenue the boys crossed, walked up the avenue, cut through the gas station on the corner, then went down Perry Street.

"If Mickey's back into drugs I've had it. My life will be over but I can't face that number. Better dead than drugs."

"You'll live," I said. "And stop trying to guess what they're up to, will you? It could be anything."

"Like what?"

"Like . . . I dunno. That's what we're trying to find out, remember?"

"Right."

The reason we didn't pursue the thought Elissa had had of other girls was 'cause basically we were what's known as secure. We both really knew that these boys were head over heels, like they say. They'd lay down their lives for us. They'd rather fight than switch. If any two boys ever loved any two girls, these guys were it.

Halfway down the block they stopped and we ducked into a doorway. Peeking out, I could see them check in all directions before they scurried like rats into an entranceway. We counted to fifty, then started down the street. We walked past the doorway they'd gone into like we couldn't care less and out of the corner of my sunglassed eye I could see that the entrance was empty. I grabbed Elissa's arm and turned her around. It was a small red-brick building with an old-fashioned wooden-and-glass door. I pushed it open. There were ten bells and about eighteen names. They might as well have been in code for all they meant to us. We decided to wait across the street until the boys came out.

At five after ten I spotted Dino and then Mickey emerging from the brick building. We'd been hanging in there for more than two hours and we hated them like poison.

We followed them all the way to The Owl on Third Street. Before we went in we stashed our disguises in our pockets. I put back my regular glasses, ran my hand through my crew cut, and we entered.

The Bonus Boys were in the back just beginning a game of pinball. As I walked toward him I eyeballed Dino good. He was about five feet eleven and real skinny. All legs. His hair was black, the bottom just brushing his shoulders. His black eyebrows were real full; they were the first thing you noticed, like two large dash marks. The eyes under those brows were brown and big and always looked sad even when they weren't. And his face was what you'd call cute.

The Mother said he was going to be real handsome when he grew up. I dunno. Maybe so. The Mother's idea, and my idea, of handsome are two different things. Gimme a blond any old day. So then what was I doing with this dark-haired Dino type, huh? And not only that, Dino was one of these macho guys. Disgusting. The thing of it was that he really wasn't. Not when he was with me alone. But when he was out in public and being a Bonus Boy, you could throw up. For instance: There he was, a cigarette tucked behind his right ear, the pack held in place by the rolled-up sleeve of his black T-shirt, his thumbs hooked inside his wide leather belt. It was the famous gangster-cowboy pose. Feh! And Mickey was no better. He was shorter by about three inches but he had big muscles 'cause he worked out. His hair was light brown, cut below his ears, and he wore wire-rimmed glasses and his mouth was always slightly open. His eyes were pale blue, like faded denim. But Mickey wasn't my problem, with his cowboy boots and his leather wristbands. Dino was.

So there they were. I ankled over to them.

"Hello, Creep," I said, tapping Dino on the shoulder.

He turned around, slow like, cool like. Then his cool was shattered and he let out a little yelp and only then did I remember he hadn't seen my hair before.

"What the hell is that?"

"It's my hair," I said.

Mickey goes, "Ya look like a plucked chicken."

"Very original," from Elissa.

"Aw, Billie, what'd ya do that for?" said Dino, sad eyes sadder.

"I just wanted to." What a nightmare this hair thing was becoming. "What'd you guys do tonight?" I asked, trying to sound casual and changing the subject at the same time.

They glanced at each other, shifty eyed, and then Dino goes, "Ah, we were just hangin' out."

"Yeah, where?"

"Around," from Mickey.

"Around where?"

"Just around. Want a Coke?" says Dino, trying to distract me.

"No. I don't drink sugar, remember?"

"Oh, yeah. Want a Tab?"

"No."

Elissa, who has never been known for her patience, suddenly goes, "You're up to something. Are you dealing again, Mickey?"

"Who? Me?" Like Mr. Innocence himself.

"Yeah, you, bigshot."

"Not me." Mickey crossed his heart with a finger.

"Me neither," said Dino.

"Then what's going on?" asked Elissa.

I could feel she was getting ready to blow our cover, so I moved in on her and gave her a light kick in the ankle.

"What makes you think somethin's goin' on?" asks Mickey.

I guess my kick was too light, 'cause after all our disguises and everything, my pal bursts out, "We followed you over to Perry Street and saw everything. Now give with the details."

Dino turned his brown peepers on me and I

felt like two feet tall. One thing we always promised each other was privacy. I didn't know what to say. The bells of the pinballs seemed to get louder and I began to sweat even though the air-conditioning was on.

Real hurt like Dino says, "You followed us?"

I nodded.

Slowly Dino shook his head, hair swinging in the breeze, like they say. He hunched his shoulders forward, pulled the cigarette from behind his ear, struck a long match against the sole of his sandal, and said, "That sucks."

"Don't try and lay a guilt trip on us for following you," Elissa yelled. "What were you doing? I'm onto these diversionary tactics. You were in that place more than two hours. Who lives there, huh?"

The guys swapped looks again, then Mickey goes, "Can't tell you."

Well, you can imagine how that went over.

Elissa narrowed her eyes, put her hands on her hips, and said, "Either you tell us or it's over between us. All of us."

See she knew, like I did, that these guys wouldn't go for that.

"Hey, wait a minute," said Mickey.

"No fair," goes Dino. "This is business and we're sworn to secrecy. You wouldn't want us to break our word, would you?"

"Yes!" from me and Elissa.

Dino scratched at his rib cage, tough, like he'd seen in some movie, then he ran a finger over the fuzz on his upper lip (he called it a mustache . . . to me it looked like dirt), popped an arm muscle, and said, "Hold it a minute, okay?" He pulled Mickey aside and they whispered, their backs to us.

We waited, tapping our toes.

Finally, they came out of their huddle and Dino said, "Okay, we'll check it out and if we can, we'll tell you."

"Listen, you bums, you think I don't know double-talk when I hear it?" goes Elissa in her best machete-mouth style.

"What double-talk?" from Mickey. "I gotta ask if it's all right to let you in on it. Get it?"

"Just tell us one thing," she said. "What you're doing, is it legal?"

They nodded, then Dino said, "Meet us tomorrow night at seven at the Garibaldi statue in the park. We'll know by then."

"It better be yes," Elissa said in a menacing tone. "C'mon, Billie."

"Hey, don't you want us to walk ya home?" from Mickey.

I opened my mouth to say okay but Elissa said no. No more contact until we knew the truth.

Elissa was tough. So I was, too.

Four

The emptiness of the loft hit me the minute I got off the elevator. Funny how you can tell when there's no one in a place. Even if The Mother had been sound asleep in her bed I would've known. But just to be sure I walked to the back of the loft and peeked in her room. Empty. Well, at least I had the cats. Three of them. There was Rita, who was a semi-longhair and orange and white; Putnam, a gray tiger; and Vivian, a beautiful calico who weighed only seven pounds. They each have very distinctive personalities, as cats do. Rita is a loner and doesn't like to be touched by us or the other cats. And she loves people food and often gets up on the kitchen counter when we're having lunch, rolls over on her back and begs, reaching out a paw for bran muffin or pasta or whatever we're eating. When my gramma was here at Christmas and Rita did that, both Arley and I screamed with shock and pretended she'd never been on the counter before! Gramma isn't a cat lover and thinks it's dirty to have cats around food. Putnam is a fourteen pounder and klutzy and needs constant love. He sits right on your

chest and eyeballs your face. And Vivian is just
about perfect. She has no bad habits. She knows
how to love you without smothering and you
can pet her. But I love them all.

I went into my room and there were Vivian
and Putnam lying on my bed. I joined them
and gave them some petting. Suddenly sugar
shot up my nose. The smell, that is. There was
a huge wholesale bakery across the street from
us, and at night when they did their baking the
sweet smell of sugar seeped into our loft filling
every crevice. Tonight it was especially strong
and it made me feel sad. Visions of fruit pies,
jelly donuts, cupcakes with vanilla and straw-
berry icing, chocolate layer cakes, and gooey
tarts sailed through my mind's eye. It was the
past when I was young. For the last five years
The Mother hasn't let us eat sugar. Sometimes I
missed it but not often. Honey desserts were
really better. Tonight I missed it. Or was it my
lost youth I missed?

Maybe it was just that thing I'd felt all my
life. A kind of sadness, or loneliness that got
into my marrow sometimes and hung around
and brought me down. I think it was because I
was an O.C. Only Child. People with brothers
and sisters always said I was lucky 'cause it was
a big pain to have to always share everything or
get hand-me-downs or have fights all the time.
But to tell you the truth, I would've put up with
any of that stuff if I could've had a sister. A
brother would've been okay but I think to have
a sister (older) would've been neat. I guess I
thought of Elissa as my sister, but I wasn't
dumb enough to think it was the same as
having a real one.

Sure, being an O.C. has advantages. When I was little I got tons of Christmas and birthday presents and The Mother and The Father paid a lot of attention to me. Too much. Sometimes I felt like I was a specimen on a glass slide.

So I was glad when they kind of backed off and left me more space for myself. But things have gotten out of hand. Being an O.C., as far as I'm concerned, has more against it than for it. There's a great big hole in my life and not much I can do about it.

As I sat there stroking the cats and feeling sorry for myself, I heard the elevator open and close, and for the first time in a long time I was glad to know The Mother was home. Maybe we could rap awhile. But I didn't want to seem too anxious. You got to train them right.

I took my time. I kissed the cats and slowly made my way down the hall and out into the living area. I stopped short. It was her all right but her "friend" was with her.

"Hi, Billie," she goes, trying to sound all perky and palsie. "I'm glad you're still up, honey. There's someone here I'd like you to meet."

My instinct was to say, "Oh, yeah, who?" but I knew it was too mean with this dude staring me right in the kisser, so I cracked a smile and kept my lips buttoned. Let her swing it alone.

"This is my friend Tom Chase."

"Hello, Billie," goes this tall red-bearded guy and sticks out a big hand.

I eyed the hand for a sec, then took it. His grip was firm. Good sign. If there was anything I hated worse than algebra it was a handshake that felt like an old flounder. "Hi," I said.

Meanwhile, The Mother was pulling at her lip with one hand and smoothing down her hair with the other. And one foot was rubbing up and down the other leg. The woman was agitated. This was the first "friend" she'd ever brought home since The Father split and I guess it was a big deal. So here was the question. Should I make it easier or harder?

"Tom's a painter," The Mother said.

"Oh, yeah?" More talent in the house.

The guy nodded.

"He's a photorealist," she went on.

"You don't say." A photorealist is an artist who paints pictures that look like photographs. I happen to like them but some people don't. So what's new?

She continued, "Tom's paintings are in the Museum of Modern Art."

"Whataya know," I said. It didn't escape me that she hadn't dragged home some business-man type. Arley was hooked on talent no matter what she said.

"He's famous," she goes.

"Oh, come on, Arley, enough," he said and laughed nervous like.

It was then that I saw it and I was just about knocked out. Braces! The guy had braces on his teeth! I couldn't believe it. This old guy, at least forty, had big shiny braces on his choppers. It made me want to laugh but I held back.

But I didn't fool him. He caught my look and he goes, "I had a bad bite and buck teeth. They'll come off in about a year."

"I never saw a grown-up with braces."

"I know," he said. "It's weird."

"Yeah, well," I said.

Then we all stood there in silence shifting and moving like we all had some nervous disorder. Finally I broke the spell. "I think I'll go to bed."

"Good night, Billie," Arley said quickly. Too quickly.

"Nice meeting you," he said.

"Right," I said.

In my room I wondered if Tom Chase was going to spend the night. I didn't like thinking about it too much so I flipped on my TV set. The news was on and an interviewer was asking a survivor of a fire how he felt when he realized his apartment was on fire. Now this drove me nuts. I mean they were always asking these kinds of dumb questions. What did the interviewer think he'd say?

"Well, Mike, when I first smelled the smoke I thought, fabulous, I think maybe there's a fire somewhere. Then when I opened my door and saw the flames shooting and leaping, I said to myself, great, that's just great, we've got a real raging fire here."

Or:

"How did you feel, Mrs. Sklar, when you knew the plane was going to crash?"

"Just wonderful, Tom. It's something I've been looking forward to for a long time."

Or:

"Were you afraid, Mr. McBride, when the robbers trained two machine guns on you in your store?"

"Oh, no, Sue, I was happy as a lark, never felt better!"

I snapped off the set.

This day had been a real bummer. First my

hair . . . a big mistake. Then the thing with Dino and Mickey. And now this Chase guy. But worst of all was that the next day I was starting my part-time summer job and nobody cared. A wish of good luck would've been nice.

I was gonna work in this Sandwich Shop down the street as a sandwich maker. My hours were eleven to three. And I was scared. Maybe you don't think there's much to being a sandwich maker—and maybe there isn't—but it's a lot to me. What if I don't put enough mustard on and a customer gets mad? What if I mistakenly give somebody capicola instead of spiced ham? And this was a fancy sandwich shop, too. Very expensive, lots of ingredients, black bread, stuff like that. Probably they didn't even have spiced ham. Too ordinary. But the thing of it was that The Mother didn't seem to care. I guess she was too involved with The Painter to remember. And naturally The Father hadn't called or anything. Too involved with The Organic Woman. Dino too, as much as he loved me, had forgotten. Well, I guess maybe that was my fault. But Elissa had let it slip her brain, too.

I climbed in under my sheet and turned off the light. Rita settled in behind my head on my second pillow. Putnam curled up near my neck and gave me the onceover. And Vivian climbed on my chest. Then she meowed long and loud for no reason at all. I smiled 'cause I knew she was saying, "Good luck on your job tomorrow."

"Thanks," I said, and closed my eyes. Vivian was a good friend.

I decided to wait to dye my hair until the afternoon 'cause I really didn't know how long it'd take and I didn't want to be late for work. The Mother, who was building a loft on Greene Street, was long gone by the time I got up. I looked around for clues to see if The Painter had stayed overnight, but I couldn't find any. Then I just had time for a muffin and a glass of milk before I left for work.

The Sandwich Shop was owned by one Jerome Oripahs who insisted we call him just Oripahs. In case you haven't already seen it, Oripahs is Shapiro spelled backwards! And in case that doesn't tell you all you need to know, I'll tell you . . . Oripahs has pretensions. Not only does the average sandwich cost three fifty to four fifty, but Oripahs himself thinks he's God's gift to SoHo on every level.

Oripahs is in his late thirties and he's already going to pouches. A sag here, a bag there. His hair is dark, thin and long. It always looks wet and you can see the comb markings. He combs it straight back, the ends just touching the edge of his white shirt collar. Every day he wears a different color bow tie and a mattress-ticking apron which is clean as can be at the end of the day.

I wouldn't say that Oripahs is exactly homely, but he's no looker, like they say. And I wouldn't even comment on his looks if he were a little, well, different. Oripahs, you see, thinks every female who walks into the store is in love with him. I knew all this before even starting work there 'cause Oscar Evans, Oripahs' other employee and the super of our building, had told me. Oscar goes to New York University, plays the guitar, and does needlepoint to relax. You should see some of his things, they're real knockouts. He's very talented. Oscar's eighteen, has hair like the end of a broom, big greenish owllike eyes, and thin lips.

So it was us three who were gonna run the Sandwich Shop for the summer during the day. Some trio.

At exactly eleven-forty-five they started coming in. I felt like I was in that movie *The Birds*. They swooped in shouting and screaming. This one wanted onion and that one wanted mushrooms and they wanted mayo and he wanted watercress and she wanted red peppers and that one asked for dill sauce while this one demanded pâté and he yelled for pickles and she screamed for capers and they slammed out!

"Is it like this every day?" I asked.

"Thank heaven, yes. Isn't it wonderful?" Oripahs said, sighing.

Oscar and I looked at each other.

"And they love me so. Did you see how that last woman, the elegant one with the diamond ring, looked me over? Embarrassing, I tell you, but they can't control themselves. Poor dears. And earlier, the one with the long yellow braid was practically vibrating, she was so taken by me. But Oripahs knows how to keep them happy." He gave a big wink. "A tap here, a touch there, a pat, a smile."

"Flirtation's your middle name, Oripahs."

Another big wink and he went into the back room. It was quarter to three and Oscar and I started cleaning up the crumbs and spilled sauces so it'd be clean for the supper crowd. I was real glad I wouldn't be there for that.

At three I gave Oscar a little pinch on the arm, waved good-bye to Oripahs, and split.

Exhausted. I walked over to the drugstore on Spring Street and picked out my peroxide for stripping out color and the dye. Purple Paramour it was called. Sounded good.

After I did the peroxide number my hair was the color of wheat. Then I mixed the dye. Even in the pot it was a shocking color. There was still time to back out but I decided to forge ahead. As I dipped in my first cotton ball, it was like my whole life danced in front of me. Well, more like all the people in it. And all of them were saying: "No, don't."

So, naturally, I did.

Five

"You couldn't have," The Mother said.

"Yeah, but I did."

"I can't believe it."

"You gotta believe it. The evidence is in!" She was, of course, talking about my hair. I gotta admit it was pretty wild. The brightest purple I'd ever laid my peepers on was what it was. And yet, it was pretty. But The Mother couldn't see the niceness of it, only the shock value.

"Can you have it fixed?"

"I don't want it fixed."

"Is something wrong, Billie?"

"Wrong?"

"Why are you doing these things? First cutting off your gorgeous hair and now dying it." She shook her head in despair.

"Why does it have to mean that something's wrong? I'm branching out, that's all."

"Branching out into what? Freakhood?"

"No. New adventures in living." I thought that sounded good.

"Spare me. All right, Billie, it's *your* hair, I guess."

"You don't have to guess. It's mine all right."

"Some comedian. Look," she goes, "if there was anything wrong you'd tell me, wouldn't you?"

"Yeah, sure."

Dessert was a plate of honey cookies and I stuffed two little ones in my mouth.

"What'd you think of Tom Chase?" The Mother asked.

"He was okay."

"Just okay?"

"Well, I didn't have any conversation with him, did I?"

I left my stool at the counter, where we'd eaten a quick dinner of burgers and salad. "I'm going out."

"Where?"

"I'm meeting Dino. Did the Chase guy stay overnight?"

Immediately she blushed. "No."

"Yeah, well. See you later."

"Billie?"

"What?"

"Would you care if he did?" She pulled at her lip.

Should I tell her I'd care or give her carte blanche? That means complete freedom. It's tough bringing up a mother. I shrugged. "Don't know. I'll think it over."

"Thanks," she goes.

On my walk to meet Elissa and the guys, a few eyes were cast my way giving my purple hair the onceover. I had to get used to it. In the park at the Garibaldi statue Elissa was waiting.

"Stunning," she goes when she sees my hair. "A stunning color."

Now that's a pal. "You think?" I said coyly, wanting more praise. Why not?

"Gorgeous. What did Arley think?"

I rolled my eyes. Enough said.

"What can you expect from old people who are also parents? No imagination. Sylvia would plotz if I did it."

"How is she, by the way?"

"She's in a good phase." Elissa smiled sadly and went on, "She's been home from the hospital four months this time. Maybe she's cured."

"Probably is," I said.

"Wouldn't that be terrif?"

I squeezed her arm. "Neat."

Her eyes changed from brown to black. "Course, you can't have everything. Andy's shooting up again."

Andy, her twin, was a junkie, a drummer, and a genius in that order, and also the favorite of the twins because he was "the boy." It was disgusting but Elissa handled it pretty good. She got all A's in school and was drug free. Still, sometimes the emphasis on "the boy" brought her down. I took her hand and squeezed hard.

"It's a miracle you stay so sane," I said.

"Yeah, I guess. Hey, how'd the job go?"

She remembered after all. "Not bad. Glad it's not gonna be my life's work, though." And then I wondered what my life's work would be? What could a no-talent like me ever do? Ah, skip it. "You start your job tomorrow, huh?"

"Some job."

She was gonna work part-time in an incense factory. Just then I looked up and saw Dino and

Mickey coming toward us. Suddenly they stopped. Gawked. Their faces were grim, like Godzilla's. "What is it?" I yelled, scared like crazy.

Dino, shaking his head, slouched over to us. "Are you nuts?"

"Me? Nuts? What?"

Elissa poked me and motioned to my head with a zap of her eyes.

"Oh, you mean my hair?" I go.

"What am I gonna do?" Dino said.

"*You* do?"

Meanwhile Mickey was doubled over with laughter. Elissa rapped him one on the head. It did no good.

"How can I go anywhere with you?" Dino asked.

"So don't," I said.

"It's stunning," said Elissa.

"A nightmare," from Dino.

Mickey kept laughing.

"Never mind my hair," I said. "What's with tonight?"

"Yeah. Is it a yes?" goes Elissa.

The Bonus Boys pulled themselves together and said that it was a yes. On the trip across the Village Dino kept walking a few steps ahead or a few steps behind me. I got the message all right. But I kept my lips zipped for the moment. I wanted to know what was up, and if I gave Dino any reason for a fight I might never find out. As it was it was thin ice, like they say.

At the Perry Street address Mickey rang the bell marked Robert Mitchell.

We waited.

Dino said, "Don't you have a scarf or something?"

"Do I tell you to shave your mustache?" I asked.

"What's that got to do with it?"

Finally the door buzzed open.

We filed in and walked to the back apartment. A man's voice called, "Door's unlocked." Just before Dino opened it he turned to me and said,

"Now don't say anything dumb."

He'll never know how close he came to getting a knuckle sandwich. I think those words were a turning point. But the sound of them faded to nothing as we walked in, because another emotion knocked my anger clear out of the ball park.

If this had been a movie, the music would have swelled real romantic and loud. Sitting in a chair was a young guy with hair the color of iced butter and a face . . . how can I describe it? I guess I'd say beautiful. Handsome. Gorgeous. But what does that tell you? One person's handsome is another person's feh! This man had brown eyes the size of quarters, a straight nose, and a mouth that was full and wide yet not too big. Just right. His chin was strong and, like a movie star's, had a cleft in the middle. As you can tell, I was spellbound. This was a mature person. Maybe in his early twenties. I thought I'd never seen anyone so neat-looking, and then he smiled and I thought I'd faint. Crinkles around the eyes! The music went on and on in my head, my knees felt like broken eggs, and the pounding in my chest, the ringing in my ears, were enough to put me out. But I stayed upright. Who was this doll?

Then Mickey introduced us all and we were told to call this beauty Mitch. Me and Elissa sat down on the couch and the Bonus Boys sort of hung against the walls looking creepy. Especially Dino. The more I looked at Mitch, the more Dino looked skinny like a snake and about as wimpy as a person could get. Nobody said anything for a bit. Mitch looked at us and we looked at him. Then he said, "Which one of you is Dino's girlfriend and which one is Mickey's?"

"Mickey is mine," said Elissa, proudly.

So two from four leaves two. Me and Dino. I wanted to yell out that Dino and I were just friends, that we barely knew each other, that we'd only now met in the hallway. But no go. It was obvious Mitch knew about us already.

"I guess you two thought maybe Dino and Mickey had some women stashed away here, huh?" He smiled.

The crinkles again, but now I noticed there was something sad about him. Something in the eyes. Not like Dino's eyes, which only looked sad 'cause of their shape. This guy's eyes were sad from the inside.

Elissa said, "Frankly, it never crossed my brain that what was happening here involved other females. Just tell me this, is it drugs?"

"Drugs?" asked Mitch.

"Yeah. Are you a dealer?"

"Cool it," Mickey goes.

"Butt out," said Elissa. "Are you dealing drugs?"

Mitch said, "No. Nothing like that."

"Is it CIA work?"

"Oh, man," from Dino.

Mitch shook his head no.

I wished I could think of something to say. My words seemed stuck in my throat and all I could do was eyeball the most gorgeous number I'd ever seen.

"What's been going on here is nothing very dramatic," Mitch said. "The guys have been building some stuff for me, that's all."

Elissa wasn't buying. "So why the cloak-and-dagger routine, huh?"

He smiled again and my heart went insane.

"I want to keep a low profile. For reasons you might not understand, I want to be in a kind of seclusion."

"You're an ex-con," goes Elissa.

"Will you can it?" said Mickey. "Hey, Mitch you want me to get them out of here?"

"It's okay. I said I'd do this and I will. I'm just not used to talking about it."

The movie music vibrated.

"You don't have to," Dino said.

"Oh, yes he does," said Elissa.

"Not if he doesn't want to," I said. I'd found my voice and suddenly they were all looking at me. "I mean, well, we're barging in and all."

"Thanks, Billie," Mitch said and tossed me a smile like a sixty-foot rainbow. "But you're not barging in. Well, here goes. I have a disease called multiple sclerosis, and the reason I'm sort of quiet about what I'm up to is...well, I guess the best way to put it is to say I want to handle it *my* way."

That was probably the bravest thing I'd ever heard.

"You don't look sick," goes Elissa.

"You don't necessarily look sick with MS. But the reason I didn't get up when you came in is that I can't without some help." He pointed to a pair of metal crutches leaning against a wall in the corner. I had been so zonked by Mitch himself I hadn't noticed them. Now it was like they were blinking in neon. Then he went on, "The guys have built ramps and railings to help me get around, and I asked them to keep it to themselves. I didn't know it was going to get them into trouble with you two."

I wanted to die. I felt like such a nerd. "I'm sorry if we caused you any trouble."

"That's okay. I can understand why you might wonder what was going on. And besides, I'm glad I got a chance to meet you."

Suddenly Dino was pulling me up from the couch. "Time to go," he said.

Me and Elissa shook hands with Mitch. I felt all tingly when our skin touched. That had never happened to me before.

"Come visit again," Mitch said.

When? I wanted to ask. How about tomorrow? Would an hour from now be too soon? But I didn't say any of that. What I said was "So long. Nice meeting you." Very original, huh?

The four of us went to Vinnie's for cappuccinos. Nobody said anything on the walk over. Sometimes it's hard to walk and talk. But this time Dino not only walked next to me, he held my hand. I hated it but I wasn't ready to make big waves. Later.

Sitting around the table, sipping our coffees, we asked how they'd met Mitch. This was the only way I could tolerate Dino...if he was talking about Mitch.

"From our ad in *The Village Voice*. Mickey got the call, right Mick?"

"Yeah, right. He calls on a Friday and we go over on Saturday morning."

"And?" asked Elissa.

Dino answered. "He told us his problem. About the MS stuff, and he said what he needed. Then Monday that week we started workin' there."

"And?"

"And he told us he didn't want anybody to know about him, where he lives or nothin'. So we promised. That's why we couldn't tell ya nothin' until we asked him. See?" Mickey wiped the steamed milk foam from his mouth with his hand.

"Use a napkin," Elissa said.

I looked at Mickey and Dino and they seemed like children. Infants. "How old is he?" I asked, holding my breath.

"Twenty-one," from Dino.

I relaxed. Not too old. A five-year difference. A drop in the bucket.

Elissa asked, "Doesn't he have a family or anything?"

Dino shrugged. "I don't know. We don't ask him a lot a dumb questions. But I can tell you this, he sure doesn't want his family to know where he is if he has one."

Then Elissa asked the million-dollar question and I thought I might pass out until Mickey answered. "How about a girlfriend? He got one?"

"Who knows? Never seen or heard of one. I think the guy's a loner. Well, you heard him. Low profile."

My heart, which I swear had stopped, started beating again. Robert Mitchell might be mine after all. Then Dino crashed through my thoughts.

"Now what are you gonna do about this purple hair, Billie?"

"What do you mean, do?"

"It's gotta go," said Dino.

It was then I realized that Mitch hadn't blinked an eye about my hair. Maybe he even liked it. Mature men were more accepting of differences. "Just what do you mean, it's *gotta* go?"

"Gotta is gotta."

Brilliant! "Here's a news flash, Dino. I'm doing nothing about it. Like it or lump it, as the saying goes."

Dino's peepers got big and round. "What's that supposed to mean?"

"Lump it is lump it."

He pressed his nonexisting lips together into a grim line. "You mean you're gonna keep it that way?"

"Smart boy."

"But why?" There was a desperate sound to his voice.

"Because *I* like it." And, I thought to myself, I think Mitch does too. "Listen, do I tell you how to wear your hair?" Maybe, I thought, this would be more to the point than the mustache number.

"That's different."

"Yeah, how?"

Shrugging and frustrated, he turned to his crony.

Mickey laid a big hand on my arm. "Hey, Billie, what's happenin'?"

"Nothing."

Mickey looked back at Dino with a raised eyebrow.

I stood up and threw sixty cents on the table. "I'm going home."

"I'll walk ya," said Dino.

I didn't want him to but felt bad for him. The child seemed so confused. So I nodded he could. "I'll see you tomorrow, Elissa. Good luck on the job. So long, Mickey."

Walking home I shoved my hands in the pockets of my overalls so Dino wouldn't try to hold one. The air was heavy and made me feel like slumping. When we got to my building Dino and I faced each other.

"This is the truth," he goes. "I hate that hair."

"You're kidding?" I said. "Here's another truth. I like it."

"Don't you wanna make me happy?" asked Dino.

Can you believe it? Some dumb dude. Even if I wanted to make him happy, which I didn't, it wouldn't be by going against my own grain. Like making my hair a boring brown again when I wanted it purple.

"You hear me, Billie?" he asked.

"Yeah."

"Well?"

"Well, I don't think we're getting along."

"In other words you don't wanna make me happy?"

"In other words I think we should call it a day," I said.

"Yeah, I think you're right."

What a wimp. He wasn't even gonna fight for me. You know how it is: even when you want something, you want the other person to protest a little. He should've said: I can't live without you. Or: please don't leave me. Instead, the creep agreed. Right away my mind flipped to Mitch and in my gut I knew he'd fight for the woman he loved.

"I have to be free," I said. "I have to be able to express myself any way I want."

"Even if it means losing me?"

I had to restrain myself from popping this egomaniac in the chops. "Yeah," I said, trying to sound like it was a fate worse than death, "even that." The sarcasm was lost on him.

"So then this is it," he goes, fooling with the fuzz above his lip.

"Guess so."

"Well, so long, Billie. I hope you get it together." He hitched up his pants, turned, and trying to look cool, arms out and swinging, he made his stupid way down the block. I've never been so glad to see the back of anyone in my life. Now I was really free. Free to think about Mitch all I wanted. There was no doubt in my mind...this was love at first sight. Why not?

Six

Three days and two nights had gone by since I'd met Mitch. I'd spent the time hanging out with Elissa, going to my job, and thinking about my new love. Usually I tell Elissa everything, but I hadn't told her how I felt about Mitch. I guess I was afraid that even my best pal would think I was crazy. It was one thing to know you were in love after a half-hour meeting and another to say it out loud. Of course if you believed in television or the movies it wasn't crazy at all. In the movies love at first sight is the normal way. The Mother always says that it's a miracle her generation is as sane as they are 'cause the movies she grew up on not only had people falling in love in thirty seconds but staying in love forever. And also the biggest disasters could happen to a person in those movies, like they could lose their house, land, mother, father, siblings in an instant, and if they shed so much as one tear, for sure someone would say, "Don't cry. Be a big girl." The Mother says that made her whole generation a bunch of repressed creeps. I dunno. My generation is encouraged to cry our brains out about every little thing, share everything that happens to us with the whole world, express every little feeling. Sometimes that makes me sick. I mean, if a guy like Mitch can swing it alone, anybody can. See, all roads lead back to him.

And there was one road I needed some help with. How to get back in to see Mitch. To get this help I was gonna have to tell Elissa how I felt about him. She was a real idea woman, and if I laid it on the table I was sure she'd come through. But that was for later. In the present was scheduled a meeting with The Father.

I hadn't seen him in a couple of weeks (no regrets on my part) so he'd called the night before. Every once in a while he remembered about me and his custody rights or something and gave a call to The Mother asking to see me. It was a big drag. Walking over to MacDougal Street, where The Father lived, I passed Captain Natoli and Pinocchio.

"Hello, young girl," he said, tipping his cap.

"Hello, Captain," I said.

Pinocchio barked, sharp and irritating.

It was three-thirty and hot as hell. Sweat was pouring down me and the stains under my arms were long and messy. I tried everything to keep from staining but nothing worked. I was wearing a short-sleeved orange shirt and there under my arms, practically to my waist, were the telltale signs of sweat. Why was sweat so embarrassing? Everyone did it. Yet those two egg-shaped marks were like signs screaming to the world that I was a bad person. I felt the same way about zits. I knew it didn't make sense but that was how I saw it.

I walked up the stairs to The Father's apartment (he called it a pad because he was still stuck in the Sixties somewhere) and knocked at his door. After what seemed like a long time he opened up.

"Oh, hiya Billie," he goes, like he had nothing to do with me being there. His black hair was pulled back into a long ponytail and he was wearing dark glasses and white painter's pants and that was all. Because of the glasses I couldn't see if he was stoned or not. The eyes always give stoned people away. "Come on in, man," he said.

We walked down a long dark narrow hallway off which was a bathroom and a kitchen. At the end of the hallway was the living room and beyond that was a bedroom. The place was dark, lit only with red lights. The walls of the living room were covered in green burlap, and there were mattresses on the floor with madras spreads on them and lots of colorful pillows. The Mother, when I described it to her, said it was "typical and juvenile."

"You want anything to eat or drink, man?"

I once asked him not to call me "man," but it was hard for The Father to keep a thought in his head. "Nothing, thanks."

"You sure, man?"

"Yeah."

"I got some pure mango juice and soybean cookies."

If there was one thing I really hated it was health food. Feh! But I didn't want to hurt his feelings so I said I'd just eaten. We sat on the mattresses facing each other and The Father lit some incense. I wondered if Elissa would be making incense that Ted would use one day.

Personally I find incense sickening, but he liked it so I didn't say anything. I really wished he'd grow up.

"So what's new?" I asked.

He shrugged his bony shoulders. "Not much, man. I got a gig tonight in Brooklyn. Wedding."

"Neat." Same old stuff.

"What's new with you, man?"

"Nothing," I said. I wondered if other girls my age had fathers they could talk to. In movies they did. If this was a movie I'd say, "Well, Dad, I've fallen in love with a man who is not only five years older than me but who has multiple sclerosis and who I've only met once for half an hour. Now what's your wise opinion, Dad?" And he'd say, "Well, daughter..." and then he'd tell me just the right thing to do. But this wasn't a movie and my father wasn't wise and grown up. Was anybody's? I guessed there were some who were more grown up than this.

I looked over at him sitting there in his lotus position, a cigarette hanging from his lips, the dark glasses hiding the windows of his soul, and I felt truly lonely.

"Could you take off your glasses, Ted?"

"Oh, hey, yeah, man, why not?"

Well, it didn't do much good because with the red lights and all I could barely see his eyes. He scratched at the hairs on his chest, some of which were turning white. "That better, man?"

"Yeah, great," I said.

"How's Dino?"

"We broke up."

"Oh, yeah? How come?"

"Bad vibes," I said. That was the kind of language he understood.

"Oh, yeah, right, man."

Then it happened. I heard the front door open and close and I knew The Organic Woman had come home. I was hoping to have this meeting go by without her but no such luck. I could hear her flopping, sandaled feet coming down the hall and then there she was. DA-DAH!

How to describe her? Well, she was tall and thin like The Father and that was okay. You can't fault a person for being tall and thin. I guess you could call her pretty, too. Big green peepers, small nose, full lips, all that stuff that models got. And she was twenty-four. The Father could've been *her* father! Anyway, today the O.W. was wearing these real short shorts made out of pink satin with a yellow stripe on each side and a red tank top and no brassiere which is okay. I mean they were hers, after all. But here's the thing. The Organic Woman had very enormous breasts, and if it had been me I would've wanted to protect them. Also I would think it wouldn't feel good without some sort of support. But the O.W. once said that to put her breasts in a bra would be like putting them in cages! She said they were her friends and she would never put her friends in cages. I don't understand people who think of parts of their bodies as separate people or whatever. Normally the O.W. had permanented curly reddish hair. Today it was...PURPLE! We stared at each other, our mouths forming little O's of surprise.

"Oh, wow," she said. She would.

"When?" I asked.

"Last week. You?"

"A few days ago."

"Oh, wow, Ted, isn't this a bummer?"

He shrugged, looked at me, noticing my hair for the first time. I wished I were dead. If there was one thing I didn't want, it was to be or look anything like Nostalgia. That's what she called herself. Nostalgia. Her real name was Mary Beth Mullendorf. Now I can see where that's quite a handle but changing it to Nostalgia? And just to a one-word name like she was famous or something. Too creepy. I guess Nostalgia didn't want to look like me either 'cause she had this expression like she wanted to kill herself. She flopped down next to The Father and stared at me, shook her head, and sighed big and loud. Then she said, "I guess it doesn't matter, we hardly hang out together."

"Right," I said.

Nobody said anything for a few minutes, and then Nostalgia said, "So, Billie, how are your feelings?"

Not How are you feeling? but How are your feelings? This was how Nostalgia talked. It was enough to make you want to throw up.

"My feelings are just fine, Mary Beth," I said.

Her lips zipped tight. "I've asked you not to call me that. If you have a problem around my name I wish you'd share it with me."

"*I* don't have a problem *around* your name, *you* do."

She sighed again and looked at The Father for some support. He was tapping out a rhythm on his leg and was lost to both of us. So back to me. "Let's not get into a hassle, okay? Just for once."

Me and Nostalgia didn't get along. Ever. I don't know why she thought this would be different. Or why she thought I'd share anything with her.

She went on, "If we want to maximize our relationship, Billie, we are going to have to humanize our attitude toward each other. We cannot have anything growthful between us if you continue in this confrontational manner. Billie, don't you realize I am your Woman-friend? Your support zone. Let's begin a new octave in our relationship. How do you feel around that?"

Can you believe it? "Nostalgia," I go, "this is how I feel over, above, and around. First off we've got no relationship. Second, you aren't my Woman-friend. And third, the only zone I'm interested in is erogenous and it's not yours!"

The Father looked up. "Hey, man, what's happening here?"

"What's happening is I'm leaving. You both make me sick."

Like they say, I beat a hasty retreat down the long dark hall, through the door, and down the stairs. Outside, the sun had sucked itself in a bit and it wasn't hot anymore. How could The Father be with her? Not that he was any bargain. Even so, I thought he could do better than Mary Beth Nostalgia Mullendorf. The Mother said Nostalgia was an ass (I also don't understand why people use parts of the body to put people down) and the only reason Ted had chosen her was because he was going through some male midlife crisis and wanted to feel young. It sounded right. Whatever it was, it didn't make me like him. Why should I go over there or see him? He didn't have anything to say or to give me. My octave with Ted James was flat. He hadn't even given me a hug. The wimp.

I made tracks over to Vinnie's. A good cup of cappuccino would calm me down. And so would seeing Elissa.

I opened the door and spotted her immediately, which wasn't hard to do 'cause Vinnie's isn't very big.

"Hi, Billie," she goes. "Guess who's here."

I walked over to her table, all the time looking around trying to see who was there but no one stood out. Same old faces. "Who's here?" I sat down and spied two cups of cap. The mystery guest was obviously in the john.

"So guess."

"Ringo Starr."

"Hilarious. Guess again."

"Miss Piggy?"

"Oh, you are a one-woman riot. C'mon, Billie."

My heart leapt in fear. "Not Dino?"

"Nah."

My heart leapt in excitement. Could it be? "Mitch," I whispered, thrilled just to say his name.

She scrunched up her face. "Who?"

"Mitch," I lovingly said again.

"What's Mitch?"

She forgot. How could it be?

"Oh, him. Nah." She eyeballed me good. Suspicion was clearly her middle name.

"I give up," I said. "Who's here?"

"It's . . ."

But before Elissa could get out the name, the mystery person was yelling from the back of the restaurant. "Yahoo, Billie, it's Tante Loco—in other words, dear heart, it's me, Aunt Ruthie from the Bronx." And then she was right up close on top of me and planting a big wet one on my cheek.

It had been a long time between kisses and it felt good. So good I burst into tears, right there in the middle of Vinnie's.

Seven

"Tzotzkalla, what's the matter?" Aunt Ruthie from the Bronx asked.

I was sitting at the table, my purple head buried in my arms, sobbing. In the occasional pause between sobs I could tell that there was a silence in Vinnie's. All eating and talking had ceased. Did I care that everyone in the joint was eyeballing me? You bet I did. But I couldn't stop bawling. Then I heard Vinnie's voice above me as Aunt Ruthie stroked my hair.

"Hey, kid, whatsamatter wit you?" he asked kindly.

It made me cry all the more.

"C'mon, Billie, tell the maitre d' whatsamatter."

Maitre d'? I peeked out from my arms at him.

He was grinning, eyes dancing. "Ya never seen a maitre d' in a T-shirt?"

I burst out in new sobs.

"Holy Moses, kid, quit it, it's bad for business. They'll think I gave ya bad food or somethin'."

Aunt Ruthie kept stroking my hair and murmuring, as though she was praying over me, and Elissa held my hand. I tried to stop and went from sobbing to crying to sniffling to short breaths.

"Better," said Vinnie. "I'll bring ya a nice cup of cap, okay?"

I nodded and finally raised my head.

"It's okay, Billie," Elissa said.

"What is it, kidlet?" asked Aunt Ruthie.

I shoved a hand in my jeans pocket, looking for tissue. None. I scrabbled around on the table for a napkin, found one, wiped my eyes, and blew my nose. Then I looked at the room at large. They were still gawking. "I'm okay," I yelled. Immediately they resumed what they'd been doing. We were all friends at Vinnie's.

Aunt Ruthie said, "Who hurt you?"

"Nobody."

"Then what?"

I shrugged. "I'm not sure. Just life, I think."

The Aunt nodded. "Ah. I know from what you speak."

That was the nice thing about Aunt Ruthie. Most adults would have said that being sixteen, I had nothing to worry about or feel sad about. They'd say these were the best years of my life. Feh! But not Aunt Ruthie. She'd never say a dumb thing like that 'cause she understood and treated us like peers. We told her our troubles and she told us hers. For instance: Aunt Ruthie was what you might call chubby and was on a perpetual diet. At least when she was at home. When she was around us, diets seemed to fly out the window. Anyway, the dieting thing was a shame because she looked sweet and pretty the way she was, all round and soft, but her husband, Marvin, wanted her to lose weight and so she tried. But she was never too successful. Once she cried to me and Elissa how Marvin caught her cheating because a piece of fried rice got stuck in her curly hair and Marvin knew she'd gone off her tuna-and-egg diet. "I couldn't help myself," she said. "Suddenly fried rice and a portion of chicken chow mein were calling out to me, and before you could say Frank Robinson I was down at the Lee Shun Foo Palace with my chopsticks flying. Somehow the telltale kernel of rice got into my locks, and when Marvin came home he zeroed right in on it. It was a holocaust, girls."

Well, we'd tried to calm her and tell her it was her body and Marvin had nothing to do with it and all that, but The Aunt wasn't into liberation. She said we didn't know what it was to have a terrific marriage, to really be in love, and if Marvin wanted her a little thinner it was the least she could do. But the point was that she talked it over with us like we were all adults.

The Aunt put her hand over mine, her many rings reflecting the light. She was very fond of jewelry and shimmered and shone around wrists, neck, and ears. Today she was wearing a matching blouse and pants of turquoise. "There's nothing special bothering you, Billie?" The Aunt asked.

Suddenly I found myself saying, "I've fallen in love."

"Yeah?" Vinnie said, leaning over me and placing my cappuccino on the table. "Who wit?"

"Don't be a yenta, Vinnie," Aunt Ruthie goes. Yenta means gossip in Yiddish.

"Why should I be different from everybody else?"

"True."

"I'm not telling the world," I said.

"Since when am I the world?" Vinnie asked.

"You don't know him," I said.

Vinnie leaned over the table and whispered, "Ya dumpin' Dino?"

I couldn't believe this. Nothing was sacred. "Please, Vinnie, I'll tell you all about it if it turns into anything. I already dumped Dino but promise not to tell him anyway." I didn't want Dino knowing my business.

"Okay. I promise. But you'll let me know what develops, right?"

"Right."

He left the table happy.

Aunt Ruthie shook her head, whispered, "The man's the biggest yenta I know."

"Who are you in love with, Billie, I'm hollishing," from Elissa. Hollishing is dying or fainting from anxiety.

Well, I'd done it. I had to tell. But I felt like a loon. "You won't laugh at me?"

Both Elissa and Aunt Ruthie reared back in their chairs, shocked and horrified, and in unison crossed their hearts with their right index fingers.

The Aunt goes, "How could you think we'd laugh at a human emotion? Especially love. I love love. I am a large reader of gothic novels, Billie, and what do you think they mostly deal with? That's right. Love with a capital L. So give. Who's the lucky fellow?"

"He's not lucky," I said. "The thing of it is, he probably doesn't know I'm alive."

"Ah, one of those."

"His name is Robert Mitchell."

Elissa started coughing and choking, smoke pouring out of her mouth and nose.

"Who?" Aunt Ruthie asked.

"Billie, are you nuts?" said Elissa, stubbing out her cig.

"You see. I knew it," I said.

"She's not laughing," The Aunt goes.

"She might as well be. She thinks I'm nuts. My pal."

"But Billie," Elissa said, "he's, he's..." She shook her head.

"What already? He's what?" asked Aunt Ruthie.

"He's older," I said.

"By how much?"

"Five years."

"Not so much," goes The Aunt. "Once I had a similar experience. I was nineteen. He was twenty-five. A Greek god he looked like. An Adonis. I worshiped him from afar for eight months." She shook her head sadly.

"What happened?"

She shrugged. "I lost him to Bambi Levine. I saw him not too long ago in the neighborhood. Fat and bald. Anyway, I understand the feeling. Now, the problem is what should you do, right?"

"Right."

"She should do nothing," Elissa said.

"Why?"

I shot her a tough look.

"Why? Because she only met him once for half an hour," Elissa said.

"A veritable stranger, huh? I see. But still you love him. Well, this is not unheard-of in the world of romance."

"Billie, you have to tell," said Elissa.

I knew she was right. "There's something else. He has multiple sclerosis."

"Ah, I see. The plot thickens. You are attracted because or in spite of?"

"Huh?"

"Do you find his disease appealing or what?"

"Well, I don't know." I thought a minute. "It would be better if he didn't have it."

"In spite of," said The Aunt.

"He needs crutches already. He's very sick," goes Elissa.

"I see. Well, that aside for the moment, what is it you want to do, Billie?"

"Well, I guess I want to see him again but I don't know how to go about it. I mean, I have no excuse to get back into his apartment. I can't just ring his bell for no reason, can I?"

"Why not?" asked Aunt Ruthie.

"What would I say?"

"Sometimes you just have to take the cow by the horns."

"Bull," I said.

"It is not bull, dear heart. A woman must take action sometimes if she wants to accomplish something."

If Aunt Ruthie wanted to think that the expression was taking the cow by the horns instead of the bull, who was I to disillusion her?

"So," I asked, "how should I go about it?"

"This is indeed a very important problem. Always, I have thought, one needs sustenance to work on these problems."

Aunt Ruthie's focus was on the blackboard above the counter where Vinnie wrote the menu.

"Vinnie," she called, "how's the homemade apple pie?"

Vinnie made a circle with his thumb and forefinger. "The best, Ru," he called back.

"A nice piece, please," she stated.

"Comin' up."

"It'll help me think," she said. "So tell me more."

"I don't know what else to say except from the moment I met him I fell. I haven't been able to think of anything else since then."

Aunt Ruthie said, "A true obsession, right?"

I nodded. "My every waking thought. In fact, almost my every sleeping thought."

Elissa clucked her tongue then lit another cigarette.

"The dreams, too, huh? That's bad business," said Aunt Ruthie.

"Here ya go, Ru, nice pie, eh?"

"Thanks, Vinnie. Looks gorgeous."

Aunt Ruthie's eyes lit up like a pinball machine. The woman really loved food. Especially dessert. I watched while she cut into the tip and took the first bite. Pure bliss spread across her face.

She swallowed. "Superb! Now I can think." So while she ate she thought. When she was finished she said, "You could pretend you were a census taker! A very great idea, if I do say so myself."

Elissa and I looked at each other. Then Elissa said, "Aunt Ruthie, he's already met her. He knows she's not a census taker."

The Aunt raised one finger in the air, pointing

upward. "Aha! He knows she *wasn't* a census taker, not that she's not, if you know what I mean."

"It's not a good idea," said Elissa.

"No?"

"It stinks," she added.

"Well, then," Aunt Ruthie goes, "I am back to square one. All right. Another idea. I think the best bet is to go to his apartment, ring the bell, and say that you've come to visit. What, I ask, is wrong with that? It's honest, it's aboveboard, and it's real. Human, too."

"You think?"

"I do."

"Elissa?"

She shrugged. "I guess."

"So what's wrong with it?" Aunt Ruthie asked her.

"The idea itself is okay. I mean, I agree. Ya just go and ya just visit, but..." She shrugged again.

"But what?" Me and The Aunt together.

"But what's the point?"

"Point? Point?" from The Aunt.

"Yeah, point. I mean, what will come of it?"

"What will come of it, she asks. So I'll tell you. What could come of it is a love affair maybe. Maybe one of the greats."

"Oh, Aunt Ruthie," Elissa said, "you're such a romantic."

"And there's something wrong with being a romantic?"

"No, I guess not. It's just that...Never mind."

"Please," said The Aunt, "do us a favor and put your cards on the floor."

"Table," Elissa said.

"Wherever. Just put them."

"Okay," said Elissa, "I will. Robert Mitchell is going to die."

"What?" I said feeling faint.

"Well that's the truth. I asked around. The end result of MS is death. And before that is worse."

"What could be worse than death?" I asked.

Aunt Ruthie said, "Plenty. But are you sure, Elissa, that MS always ends that way?"

"That's what I heard."

"Well, I don't care," I said. "I love him and maybe we can have something before." My glasses seemed to be fogging so I took them off and wiped them clean on my shirt.

"First of all," goes The Aunt, "it depends on what the *something* is, if you know what I mean, and secondly what does this Mr. Mitchell think of the purple hair, may I ask?"

"Aunt Ruthie," Elissa said in a warning tone.

"I know, I know, but I'm just wondering."

From this exchange I knew my hair had been discussed before I'd arrived. I'd wondered why The Aunt hadn't commented. She was, after all, the commenter of the world.

"So?" she asked again, openly eyeballing my hair.

"So he said nothing."

"The polite type, huh? Well, that's nice, but I think you should get rid of the hair coloring before seeing him again."

"I disagree. This," I said, running my fingers through my crew cut, "is me."

"You're sure this is you?" Aunt Ruthie asked.

"I am."

"Okey doke. I guess you should know who is

you. Personally, I think it looks like you're a maniac, but then, what do I know, right?"

We didn't answer.

She went on. "So, I think action is in order and I agree that death is not to be considered. I'm not even sure that's correct. I'll look it up at my favorite library, which is right next to Harriet Laine's Bake Shoppe. Oh, the cookies. Well, never mind that. To continue. The age difference is immaterial. After all, you're not planning marriage, are you?"

"No." At least not right away.

"So there. It doesn't matter. As for the *something* you referred to, I hope you'll be sensible. I know I'm old-fashioned on these matters but sometimes old-fashioned is best. Whatever, use your head, kid. Enough said. So when will you visit him?"

"How about next week?" I answered, suddenly feeling very afraid.

"How about now?" Aunt Ruthie said. "We'll walk you. Vinnie, the check, please."

"Now? Oh, I can't. I gotta go home, and besides what if Dino's there?"

"Dino doesn't go over until night," Elissa said.

"Yeah, but..."

"No *yeah buts*. You'll go, you'll ring, you'll see, you'll talk, you'll leave."

It sounded easy put that way. "All right," I said meekly.

"Good."

"I'm not for it but I'll walk you anyway," from Elissa.

All the way over to the Village I felt sick. I kept thinking of excuses to turn back but, naturally, Aunt Ruthie wouldn't let me. Elissa was quiet but The Aunt kept talking, trying to give me courage. My mind filled with *what ifs*. What if he didn't remember who I was? What if he remembered but wouldn't let me in? What if he let me in but was mean to me? And so on. By the time we got to his building I was shaking and feeling sick to my stomach.

"I can't," I said, practically doubled over with terror and nausea.

"You can. It's all in your mind," said Aunt Ruthie.

"It's in my belly."

"Be proud," she said. "Unless he's a putz he'll be happy to see you. After all, darling, who wouldn't be happy to see you?" She smiled, her eyes filled with love.

I didn't want to tell her that I could think of a dozen people who wouldn't want to see me. Let her have her illusions! "Maybe he's resting," I said lamely.

"Even so. Go, sweetheart, ring."

I took a deep breath. "All right."

"Good girl."

She kissed me on both cheeks like I was a soldier going into battle.

Elissa shook my hand. "Good luck, pal."

"We'll wait five minutes. If you're not out by then we'll go."

"Okay."

"Break an arm," said Aunt Ruthie.

Leg, arm, what was the difference? Good luck was good luck and I needed all I could get. I opened the outside door and stood in the small entranceway staring at his bell. I counted to three and pushed. I waited. And waited. I remembered that it might take him a bit to get to the answering bell. It seemed forever. Then his voice came through the intercom.

"Who is it?"

"Billie James."

"Come in," he said, and rang the buzzer to open the door.

I couldn't believe it. He knew who I was. My heart was pounding and my knees knocking, but even so, I was glad I'd taken the cow by the horns.

Eight

He was standing at the door on his metal crutches, the loops around the upper parts of his arms. It was a shock to see him that way, since I'd only seen the guy sitting down. Sitting in a chair you never would have known the difference. But now it was loud and clear. Still, he was smiling, making those crinkling lines around his eyes, and the cleft in his chin seemed deeper and sexier than the first time I saw him. Right above my belly button I felt something like a long ping!

"Hello, Billie," he said, "how nice of you to come by." He leaned into the loop on his right crutch and extended his hand for a shake.

Trembling and sweating, I gave him my hand. "It's hot out," I said, dumbly referring to the slipperiness of my palm.

"Well, I have air conditioning so you'll cool off soon. Make yourself comfortable." He shut the door behind me and I inched my way into the room. Slowly he turned around, then made his way, leaning heavily on the crutches, over to his chair.

It was painful to watch him. He moved so

slowly. I wondered if it hurt. At the chair it took him almost a minute until he was able to sit down, his crutches leaning against a rack that had obviously been made by Dino and Mickey.

Looking at him, I couldn't believe that he might die soon. How could it be? It was bad enough that this terrific guy had multiple sclerosis and that it had done this to his legs. I suddenly felt mad. But mostly what I felt was that I was in the presence of someone wonderful. There was something special about Mitch. Most guys seem like they have some kind of screen around them and they're all gruff and thorny. Mitch gave out an essence of rounded corners and open windows even though he was very masculine. But there was a feminine quality to him which was real neat. I think we all have both sides, but most of us are afraid to show it, especially males. I guess that was it. He didn't seem to be afraid to show his feminine side.

"There's some soda in the refrigerator if you'd like a cool drink."

"No thanks," I said, knowing there would be no way I could swallow noiselessly in front of him. As it was I felt real creepy, sitting there on his striped couch like I was this huge ugly monster with not one thing to say.

"Did you think you might find Dino here?"

"Oh, no. I know he comes over at night. Dino and I are—well, we're just friends." My glasses felt like they weighed six hundred pounds on the bridge of my nose. I wondered how Mitch felt about girls who wore glasses.

"I thought Dino was your boyfriend. The other night . . ."

"We broke up," I interrupted. I wanted him to know I was available.

"I'm sorry," he said.

"You don't have to be. I did it."

"Then I'm sorry for him." He smiled that smile and I thought I might die.

Besides, what did he mean, he was sorry for *him*? It could only mean one thing. If he was Dino and I broke up with *him* he'd be blown away! There was definitely hope for me and Mitch.

"You mean you just came by to visit *me*?"

I nodded.

"How come?"

The only thing that could've made me happy at that moment was if the floor had opened up and swallowed me. That's what I wanted. To disappear, vanish, be seen no more! But there I sat. An enormous hulk, filling his couch, not knowing what to do with my hands and feet, knowing my purple hair was blinding him, disgusting him. "How come?" he had asked. A simple question, you say. He might as well have asked me to explain the theory of relativity. What could I say? I came by because I've fallen desperately and madly in love with you? Could I say "just because" like some inarticulate child? Help, I wanted to shout, but who to or what to, I didn't know. I was getting nowhere and hours, it seemed, were passing.

"Billie?" he said, cocking his head to one side.

"Oh, sorry," I said. "I came by because I thought . . . because I . . . well, it was like this, I . . ."

"Did you think I might be lonely?"

I jumped at this idea and nodded my head like a crazy puppet.

"That's nice," he said. "I do get lonely sometimes. Thank you."

"Don't you have any friends?"

"I'm new to New York."

"Where are you from?"

He stalled around for a second or two, then said, "California."

You know the expression, takes one to know one? Yeah, well, though I've given up my lying career, I can still spot a fabrication when I hear one, and there was no way Robert Mitchell was from sunny Cal. At one time Liar had been my middle name so catching his lie was real easy for me. But he had the right to tell me whatever he wanted, and I didn't think I had any business confronting him, so I said, "I've never been there. Is it nice?"

"It's all right. I like New York better though. Not that I've seen much of it."

"How come?"

"Well, I haven't gone out too much. I don't get around very easily with those." He waved a hand at his crutches and I noticed a set to his mouth I hadn't seen before. It was as if he'd tasted something bitter. Maybe he had.

I took another cow by another horn. "I could show you around."

"You mean *help* me around, don't you?" He looked very serious.

Had I? I chewed on it a sec and realized I'd meant both. But before I could answer Mitch was speaking again.

"Billie, I want to ask you a question, okay?

Please try and answer me truthfully because it's very important to me."

"Okay."

"Do you feel sorry for me?"

Well, you can imagine that the question knocked me for a loop. I mean, most people don't ask you that question. But then most people don't have MS. I knew he wanted me to say I wasn't sorry for him but I was in a way. Why wouldn't I be? "Well, I am and I'm not."

"Meaning?" His brown eyes looked rich.

"Meaning I'm sorry that a young guy like you has got this disease but I don't pity you."

He smiled and a look of relief came over his face. "I think we can be friends."

"I'd like that."

"Just don't ever pity me, okay?"

"I won't." I wanted to ask him if that meant I could never help him or go with him outside, but I decided to hold my questions until I knew him better.

But he didn't hold his questions. "What made you dye your hair purple?"

I couldn't tell if he liked it or hated it. "I thought it would be fun."

"Is it?"

The truth was that not one thing about it had been fun. I'd had practically nothing but put-downs since I'd done it. But I didn't want to tell Mitch that, so I said, "I like it."

He nodded. "Well, that's what counts."

Then I heard myself saying, "Dino thought it was a bummer."

"Is that why you broke up?"

"Well, it was the straw, if you know what I mean. Dino's a nice kid but very immature."

"They say girls are more mature than boys at your age. How old are you?"

"I'll be seventeen." No need to add that it wouldn't be for seven months.

"Sweet sixteen, huh?" He smiled.

I tried to smile back but I was feeling too icky. Talking about my hair was preferable to my age so I switched back. "The thing about Dino is he cares too much what others think. My philosophy is that what other people think of me is none of my business. So I do what I like." I pointed to my hair.

"That's a healthy attitude."

I had to know what he thought about my purple hair and he didn't seem to be volunteering an opinion. Another cow, another horn. "What do you think of my hair?"

He raised his thick eyebrows. "I thought you didn't care what other people thought?"

Boy, I sure had walked into that one. I wanted to die. I tried to recover. Shrugging casually, I said, "I don't. But I was just curious."

"Well, let's see. I don't think I'd ever dye my hair purple but then we're not the same person. Thank God. But since it makes you happy I think it's fine that you did it. As long as a person knows the real reason why they do something that's a little unusual, I think it's great."

"The real reason?"

"Sure. It's always good to know *why* we do things. Now, tell me all about yourself. Where you were born, who your parents are, you know."

For a second my mind was still on the "real reason" stuff, and then I let it go 'cause he was giving me that great smile. Well, I stayed for another hour and I flapped and flapped about myself. It was neat having somebody so interested in me. Then, when I was getting ready to go, I realized I didn't know anything much about him 'cause I hadn't asked and that wasn't like me so I said as much.

"Oh, that's okay," he said. "Next time. Do you play backgammon?"

"No."

"Would you like to learn? It's a good game."

"That'd be neat."

"I'll teach you. Why don't you come over tomorrow after your job. Unless you have something better to do."

Something better to do? He had to be kidding! "I'll be over," I said.

"Good."

We shook hands good-bye, and I was sure he held my hand just a second more than was necessary.

At home with The Mother at dinner, I found it hard to focus in on what she was saying. I couldn't think of anything but Mitch. His eyes, his smile, the cleft in his chin. And my stomach wasn't in such great shape either. I would've sworn there were a thousand pairs of little feet tap-dancing inside me. Also, playing in my mind was the tape of that afternoon. I heard every word we'd said over and over and over again. And I wasn't bored for a sec.

"Billie, are you listening to me?" I finally heard The Mother saying.

"Yeah, sure."

"No you're not. Your eyes are all glazed. Hey,

you're not on something, are you?" She put down her fork, fear giving her a pinched look.

"Course not," I said. "I don't do drugs, you know that."

She nodded. "So what is it then? I can tell something's up."

You know, it would've been nice to tell her. The way it was sort of soothing to talk to Aunt Ruthie about these things. But she would've gotten uptight about it. Too old for you, she'd say. And I could just imagine what her reaction would be to him having multiple sclerosis. I didn't want to be hassled so I said, "Nothing's up." I didn't consider that a lie. To me it was just a survival tactic.

"Oh, Billie. You really take me for some kind of fool, don't you?"

She had a point. One thing I'd learned in this life was that Mothers did know when something was going on with you. I knew that to keep saying there was nothing wrong was gonna get me nowhere. So I quickly came up with what would satisfy her best. "I saw Ted and Nostalgia today."

"Ah," she said, already easing. "Bad, huh?"

"Yeah, well, you know how it is," I said. "He was stoned and The Organic Woman was giving me one of her psychobabble raps."

The Mother nodded wisely, understandingly, and as far as she was concerned we were pals again. Conspirators in the never-ending battle against the childishness of The Father. But the truth was that even though he was a jerk, he was still my father and I wished he was different, and as much as Arley Carpenter might've thought I enjoyed putting him down with her, I didn't. Still, I didn't have the courage, or whatever it took, to tell her that. Ripping the O.W. apart was another matter. This I enjoyed and it did bring me and The Mother closer together, but that only lasted for a short while as those things do. Negative stuff, I've found, is a bond that is not lasting, and even when the person you are putting down deserves it, like Mary Beth Mullendorf, the energy that it takes to do a hatchet job eventually drains you or something and leaves you feeling empty and maybe even a little depressed. At least this has been my experience. The strange thing is the opposite is just as true. Saying something real nice about somebody, spending time talking about the nice things about a person, may not get you as high momentarily, but it'll last longer, the feeling of niceness, that is, and it's more solid. It doesn't turn against you. Nevertheless me and The Mother spent a good ten minutes zapping it back and forth over the body of one Nostalgia.

We're not saints, after all!

Nine

Elissa came into the Sandwich Shop just before I was due to be released from that insane asylum, and stood near the doorway giving me hand signals like she was playing charades, and I, who was never good at the game, understood nothing. I gave back one of my own signals to cool it until I got off work and she stepped outside to wait.

Inside, Oripahs was droning on about this woman and that woman, all of them in love with him. Oscar and I went about our business giving perfunctory grunts so the boss would think we were listening. One horrifying thing, by the way. Oripahs *loved* my hair! That gave me pause, like they say. If that phony fool liked it, what could it mean?

At three o'clock I said my good-byes and joined Elissa on Prince Street. "What's up? You look wacko."

"Thanks. You look terrif, too."

"Well, you're giving me all these signs like some maniac, what am I supposed to think?"

"You're supposed to decipher and interpret."

"So, I'm a bust at codes, what can I say? Tell."

"Dino Farelli is a missing person!" Elissa said, eyes wide and signifying drama.

What could this mean? "Elaborate, please."

"He didn't go home last night and nobody knows where he is."

We had been walking down Prince and now we were at the door to Vinnie's. I stopped. "Cappuccino?"

"Why not?"

Inside, the regulars occupied their tables and Benny the Bookie was taking money from a table of women who were betting the numbers. Numbers had something to do with horse racing, was definitely illegal, and I didn't understand how it worked. Vinnie once said he'd explain it to me, but not being a gambling person I declined the offer. All I knew was that Bennie, who was a man in his late fifties and who always wore a hat called a trilby (like detectives in movies wear), sometimes made people happy and sometimes made them sad. Also, he never smiled and continuously looked over his shoulder. I thought his life was not a satisfying one.

"Hello, young girls, howa you?"

"Just fine, Captain Natoli," I answered, sitting down at a back table. "And you?"

"My son anda my daughter gonna visit me today. Later on."

I felt real bad. As I said before, the Captain's children were all dead. Maybe he meant his grandchildren. "You mean your grandchildren, Captain?"

"Oh, no. My son Adolpho and my daughter Yolanda."

Vinnie came up behind the Captain and shook his head. I'd never seen him look so serious.

Elissa said, "That's nice, Captain. You'll have a good time with them."

"That'sa right, young girl, a good time."

He drifted off toward the front, holding Pinocchio in his arms.

Whispering, Vinnie said, "It's finally happening. Senile, I think. Always before he talked about the past, but now the past's the present, know what I mean?"

"He thinks his children are alive?" I asked.

"Yeah. We gotta humor him. It's all we can do."

"But won't he feel rotten when Adolpho and Yolanda don't show?" asked Elissa.

Vinnie shrugged. "Who knows? Maybe he'll forget he thinks they're gonna visit or maybe he'll snap out of it, but trying to bring him into reality ain't gonna help, I don't think."

"I think you're right," Elissa said. She had a lot of experience with people straying from reality.

"You want two caps?"

We said yes and Vinnie went to get them. I turned to Elissa. "So what's this all about, this missing persons number?"

"What can I tell you? He didn't go home last night and his mother called all over the nabe this A.M. looking for him. Hey, she didn't call you?"

"Nope." Then I remembered I'd heard the phone ringing but I was into a dream about Mitch and didn't want to really wake up.

"Dino's never done this before. Home late,

yes, but never out the whole night without phoning or something."

"She called the police?"

Elissa nodded. "They say a person has to be missing twenty-four hours before they're missing."

"Typical. Missing is missing, I say."

"That's what Mrs. Farelli said to the police, but they didn't agree. Anyway, the search is on. Mickey's got a bunch of guys looking in all the possible spots. I, for one, think Dino's split the scene."

Vinnie put our cappuccinos on the table. "Ya look seriously engaged," he said. "Something up?"

"Dino's disappeared. Missing since three yesterday afternoon," said Elissa.

"No kiddin'. Want I should put up a poster or somethin'?"

"Let's wait on that," I said.

"So leave me know if there's something I can do, okay?"

"Right."

When Vinnie was gone Elissa asked, "Do you care at all?"

"About Dino? Of course. I mean, I don't want anything to happen to him. But what did you mean you think he split?"

"My opinion is that he's got a broken heart and he's gone on the road to get over you. Actually, this is Aunt Ruthie's opinion. I checked her out on the subject since she's a guru on romance. She says Dino is grieving for you."

I sipped my cap. "My opinion is that you and Aunt Ruthie are crackpots. Dino broke up with me as much as I broke up with him. He hated my hair and didn't want me to be me, and to express myself, so we parted company. It was a two-way street."

"Not according to Mickey."

"What do you mean?"

"Dino said he knew you were getting ready to dump him and so he pretended he wanted to end it too. But he really loves you, hair and all."

"He's got a funny way of showing it," I said.

"Well, he'll turn up. I'm not worried. So, you want to know about Mitch or not?"

"Ohmigod, I forgot!"

I filled her in with all the details. Elissa and I loved details. And then I said, "As a matter of fact, I'm late now. He's gonna teach me how to play backgammon."

"Billie," she said, sounding serious, "do you think you're in love?"

I could feel the blood rushing up my neck and bursting into my cheeks. "I think so."

"I thought that's what you'd say. Well, I'm your pal and if he's who you want then I'm for it, but I gotta say, as your pal, I think you're asking for a whole bunch of trouble." She stubbed out her cigarette.

"I know what I'm doing," I said.

"I hope so."

We paid our check and left. At the corner of Prince and Sixth Avenue we were preparing to part when I spied Captain Natoli and Pinocchio standing in the middle of the avenue. The light changed and horns started honking and cars started whizzing around him. Drivers screamed at him from their open windows:

"Get off the road, you old creep."

"Are you crazy? Take that mutt and beat it."

"Go on, get back to your nursing home."

People were so rotten sometimes. I opened my mouth to yell to him, but Elissa grabbed my arm.

"No, wait until the light changes and the cars stop. He might try to come back to us and get hit."

She was right. We waited. It was a heart-stopping sight. Each second seemed like a year. Finally the light changed. "Captain Natoli," I yelled.

He turned, his small body like a child's, the big officer's cap held up by his Dumbo-like ears. His eyes, faded with age, suddenly sparked. "Oh, young girls," he said, "hello, hello." Slowly, with Pinocchio in his arms, he started toward us as we started toward him. Elissa took one arm and I the other. Moving very slowly, we finally got him safely to the sidewalk.

"What were you doing in the middle of the street, Captain?"

I guess I sounded angry because his tan eyes filled with tears. I felt awful. "Oh, don't cry," I said. "I'm not mad."

"No, no." He shook his head as if he was very tired. "I try to go home to wait for my chillern."

"But you don't live this way, Captain," said Elissa.

And with that he really started to cry. The tears slid down his wrinkled cheeks and Pinocchio, his tongue making feeble attempts, tried to lick them away.

"What is it?" I asked.

"I no remember where I live," he said, still crying.

Elissa and I looked at each other. I felt like

crying myself and I knew she did too. The old man was completely disoriented and afraid. And maybe even ashamed.

"It's okay," I said and stroked his arm.

"Yeah, it's okay. We'll take you home."

Well, it was a real moment of truth. Elissa was my pal, and when things got tough we always stuck together, helped each other. I had always hated girls who broke dates with their friends just 'cause a guy came along and this was kind of a similar situation. I wanted like crazy to go over to Mitch's and I knew he was waiting for me but my friend needed me. Sure, she could take the Captain home alone but I knew in my heart she didn't want to. I wouldn't have wanted to. This was something you did with someone else. It wasn't just a matter of taking him to his building. It was important that he be taken to his apartment and given something to drink maybe and also given a little love. But seeing Mitch was important too.

"You can split, Billie," Elissa said, as always reading my mind. "I can swing it alone."

I thought she sounded sincere. Still. "No, it's okay, I'll go with you."

She shook her head, black curls jiggling. "I know you got a date. It's cool."

"Really?"

"Sure."

I felt just like I was being ripped in half, a zigzag line down my middle. "You'll have to take him upstairs."

"I know. Go on."

"You're sure?"

"Yup."

"Captain Natoli," I said, "you do everything Elissa here tells you, okay?"

"Sure, young girl. You nicea girls to me. I just mix up."

"You'll be okay now." I looked deep into Elissa's eyes to try and see the real truth.

She said, "What're you looking for, gold? Take off."

I had to believe her. "I'll call you later."

"Right."

I turned around and at the corner I headed up Sixth Avenue toward the Village and Mitch. My feet felt like lead, my heart like coal. And I was sure the knots in my belly had been tied by a sailor. How come, if I was doing the right thing, I felt like such a mess? I thought of Mitch and little thrills of love rippled over me. And then I thought of Elissa taking the Captain home all by herself. Was I crazy? I had some nerve to call myself a friend. But Mitch. But nothing. Right before I reached King Street I twirled like a top and ran back down Sixth and turned the corner into Prince, where I stopped.

They'd hardly made any headway at all. Pinocchio was on the ground now, walking as slowly and stiffly as his owner. Captain Natoli had his arm through Elissa's and I could see that he was talking. I quickened my step and soon was beside the Captain, slipping my arm through his frail one.

"Hi," I said, "going my way?"

"Oh, young girl, you back." When the Captain grinned it looked like a woodcut.

"What're you doing?" Elissa asked.

"I'll see Mitch later or tomorrow. I can do that

any old day. You don't mind if I come along, do you?"

"I guess not," she said, her dimple starting to peek through her cheek.

"You very nicea young girls. I give you hot choc when we get home."

Being that it was about eighty degrees out I said nothing.

"Don't worry about anything anymore, Captain. Me and my pal here will take good care of you," Elissa said and gave me a big wink.

Everything in me relaxed and I knew I'd made the right decision. You can't always do everything you want. Sometimes you have to give a little.

Captain Natoli lived in an apartment house on Thompson Street between Prince and Spring streets. Not everything in SoHo had turned chic! There were still these inexpensive places where a lot of people had lived for years and years, some of them all their lives. The Captain himself had been in the same place for about thirty years, ever since his wife died.

"What floor are you on, Captain?" Elissa asked.

"Floor? What you mean, young girl, what floor?"

"We don't know where you live," I said.

"Oh, mia casa. I show you."

The hallway was dark and long but clean. At the back were the stairs. No elevator here. We started climbing. I couldn't believe that this old man had to climb like this. And Pinocchio too. But the Captain didn't seem to give it a thought. To him it was an everyday occurrence, like brushing your teeth. We went up five flights. Count 'em . . . five! Elissa and me, we were out of breath by the time we got to the sixth floor, but the Captain and Pinocchio seemed in fine shape.

"Back here, young girls."

We followed down the dark hall to his apartment. From his pocket he took a key and opened the door. The smell hit my nostrils right away. Not that it was a bad smell, no garbage or anything, but it was musty. Once when I'd visited my gramma in Ohio and I'd gone up into her attic, I'd smelled that same smell. But this was where a person lived, not some old attic.

We went inside and found that the place was stuffed with furniture. Not the kind you see much anymore either, but the old kind, dark, big, heavy. I guess it was antique, but to my eye not pretty. It was too big and overpowering, especially in this small living room. I knew, of course, that these ugly pieces were from the Captain's past and must've meant a whole lot to him.

"What a nice place you got here, Captain," I said. Elissa and me exchanged a look conveying our true sentiments but naturally we didn't let him see.

"Thank you, young girl. This my home. I live here long time. But before that I live in biga house with my bride Concettina and all my chillerns. She gone now. They alla gone." His face grew very sad.

I felt awful for him. Well, at least he wasn't expecting Adolpho and Yolanda anymore. He looked limp standing there in the clothes that always seemed too big for him, so I thought I'd change the subject. "How about the hot chocolate you were gonna make us?" It was about ninety degrees in the apartment. My stomach whirled at the thought of a hot drink. "Can I open a window, Captain?"

"Sure thing," he said, sounding sprightly again. Every once in a while the Captain used funny expressions like "sure thing," which he probably picked up around the neighborhood. It sounded odd coming out of his mouth.

Elissa poked me and pointed to a piece of the massive furniture. I think it was called a sideboard. Now that the blind was up and the window open I could see better. There must've been two inches of dust covering everything. No wonder it smelled musty.

"I think we better do something about this horror show," said Elissa.

"Huh?"

"Clean, dummy, clean."

"You think?"

"I know."

She was right. Something had to be done. It couldn't be healthy for him to live in all that dust.

"Come in here, young girls," he said, walking toward the kitchen. "Nicea hot choc."

My heart trembled a little as I went in, 'cause I figured if the rest of the place was such a mess what would his kitchen be like. But I was pleasantly surprised. Spotless. Somehow the Captain had managed to take care of the kitchen.

He opened a cabinet, looked in, closed it. There were four cabinets and he did the same with each one. Then he stood in the middle of the kitchen, looking confused and upset.

"What's wrong?" from Elissa.

"I no unnerstan'."

"What?"

"No hot choc."

"I'll look," said Elissa.

She started opening and closing cabinets and by the third one she turned to me, her face the color of rice paper, her eyes all droopy.

"What's wrong?" I asked.

"He's right. No hot choc."

"So what?" Personally, I was relieved.

"No nothin'."

"What do you mean?"

She motioned me over with a jerk of her head. Then she opened the first cabinet. Empty. Second. Empty. The third held a huge set of dishes and glasses and the fourth was halfway stocked with dog food. But there was not a sign of human food anywhere. Both of us had the same idea at the same time and went for the fridge. Elissa got there first and opened it.

There was one can of opened dog food, a bottle of ice water, and one old onion growing long green horns. She closed the door.

The Captain was still standing in the middle of the kitchen, looking bewildered.

"Captain Natoli," I said softly, "don't you ever eat at home?"

"Whata you say?"

"Where do you eat your meals?"

"I eata here with Pinocchio," he answered, smiling and beaming happiness that he had such a nice dining companion.

It hit me then. I'd seen reports on television about it but never paid too much attention. Now it came back to me as if it had been stored away for just this occasion. "Let's go sit in the living room, okay?"

"That'sa good," he said.

When we were all seated, me and Elissa on a lumpy couch and the Captain in a big easy chair with Pinocchio on his lap, I brought the food thing up again. "Captain, do you mean you eat Pinocchio's food?"

Elissa twirled her head, eyeballing me like I was nuts or something.

He pressed his thin lips together and slowly his head nodded out a yes. "I heat her uppa nice," he said.

"Oh, God," said Elissa.

"It'sa good for me."

I swallowed a batch of sadness and went on. "You get a check every month, don't you? A Social Security check?"

"Yeah. He come every month. You wanna see my bride?" He reached out and opened a cardboard box that was on the table next to him. From it he took a picture and held it out to us. Elissa got up and took it from him and brought it back to the couch. It was a beautiful young woman in a blouse and a long skirt. Her hair was pulled up and back and there was a smile on her face. The picture was tinted brown.

"That'sa Concettina, my young girl, my bride." His eyes were lit now, bright and sparkling like I'd never seen them.

"She's real pretty," said Elissa.

"Gorgeous," I said.

He nodded, pride puffing out his thin old chest. He'd gotten me off the subject of food, but I knew I had to get to the bottom of this. So even though I understood he didn't want to talk about it I went right back. "Captain, what do you do with the money from the check?"

He shrugged. "I pay alla bill."

"Don't you have any left over for food besides Pinocchio's?" asked Elissa.

"We share the samea food. No talk this no more." A look of anger crossed the Captain's face and we understood that his dignity was at stake.

"Excuse us a minute," I said to him. I pulled Elissa up from the couch, into the hall. "We gotta do something," I whispered.

"You said it."

"You got any money?"

"Forty-five cents. You?" asked Elissa.

"I'm flat. I don't get paid until Friday."

"Me too. You think Vinnie'd loan us?"

"Maybe."

Then Elissa's eyes seemed to roll around their sockets like they were oiled. "Hey, I got an idea."

"No kidding."

"I think this is a problem for Aunt Ruthie from the Bronx!"

"I think you may be right." Not only was Aunt Ruthie sympathetic to all our problems but she was also, like they say, loaded. I pictured her in a telephone booth changing from her everyday clothes into her Superaunt costume. "Call her," I said.

So Elissa went downstairs to call Aunt Ruthie while I returned to Pinocchio, who was snoring, and Captain Natoli, who was not. In his hands he held some more pictures.

"Adolpho and Yolanda," he said, proudly holding the pictures out to me.

I pulled over a wooden chair and sat real near the old man. "Show me all the pictures," I said. "I love pictures."

He smiled broadly, showing tiny little teeth with some gold fillings. I settled down to wait for Elissa's return, and for a moment I thought of Mitch and wondered if maybe he might be thinking of me. I hoped he didn't feel I'd abandoned him. I guessed he needed company as much as the Captain but it was different somehow. On this day his situation wasn't as desperate as the Captain's. Priority was the key word here.

And even though my heart said priority was on Perry Street with Mitch, my mind told me that the truth was priority was here. A very old man needed some help and I could maybe give it. Just then the Captain leaned over with another picture and planted a big kiss on my cheek.

"You sucha nicea girl," he said.

"You're nice too." I kissed him back.

Then I wondered how long it had been between kisses for this old man. Maybe I wasn't doing so bad after all.

Ten

It was six o'clock when Elissa and I left the Captain's. Vinnie had lent us ten bucks and Elissa had shopped for some food. Ten dollars sure didn't go far. We made the old man a hamburger and a potato and some string beans before we left and told him that we would be there in the afternoon the next day with Aunt Ruthie from the Bronx, who had promised to come in with some money and some ideas.

I was surprised to find The Mother at home and scurrying around the kitchen like something out of a sit-com. Frankly, she looked nuts. Her hair was up in these ugly rollers (I'd never seen this trip before), there was some kind of goo on her face, and her eyes said panic.

"What is it?"

"What's what?" She pulled at her lip, indicating nervousness.

"What's going on?"

"Nothing."

"Well, what are you cooking?"

"Cornish game hens."

I walked over to the counter and saw these two sweet little birds in a pan.

"Tom is coming to dinner," The Mother said.

Now it was starting to add up. A sensible woman like Arley James was going to pieces because some man was going to eat her cooking. Go figure it.

"Well," I said, "I don't think I can eat those birds. Too cute."

"Good, because you're not going to."

"Huh?"

"This is a private dinner. You can eat something now. He's coming at seven-thirty. There's last night's leftovers in the fridge. Heat them up."

"Thanks." It's one thing to not *want* to do something and another to be not wanted. A big dull thud hung in my stomach.

"Please, Billie, don't act pitiful. I have a date and I want to have it alone. Another night you can eat with us."

"So who wants to?"

"Look," she said, "what's so terrible? Do I go along on your dates with Dino?"

She had a point but I wasn't going to let her know it. "Me and Dino broke up."

"Dino and I," she corrected.

She didn't even care. I thought maybe she'd wonder why or how or something but she didn't notice or care. Her only interest now was The Painter and her Cornish hens.

Suddenly I wasn't hungry. "I'm going out."

"But you haven't eaten. Billie, please don't make it more difficult than it is."

"Why is it difficult?"

"I don't know. It just is."

Standing there in the middle of the kitchen, hair

in rollers, face in goo, she looked pathetic, like something from a freak show. I sort of felt sorry for her. The Painter was the first man she'd seriously dated since The Father split. Maybe she was scared. It never occurred to me that if grown-ups had dates they might get all creepy and scared. I remembered back to when I had my first couple of dates with Dino. It was horrible. I was in a sweat all the time, thinking I smelled like a skunk. And I always felt sick to my stomach.

"You feel like you're gonna throw up?" I asked her.

"No. Why?"

"Just wondered."

"Do I look like I'm going to throw up?" The Mother asked.

"Who can tell?"

"It's just face cream," she said.

"Beauty cream?" I mocked.

"Please don't."

The sound in her voice was weird. Like maybe she might cry. She was scared all right. Well, she didn't want sympathy from me, that was for sure. Let her handle her own problems. Who was the mother here anyway?

"I'm going out."

"What about your dinner?"

"Not hungry." I pushed the button for the elevator. Rita was hanging around my feet, brushing her red furry coat against my legs like she wanted me to take her with me. "Beat it, sister," I said to her. Tough as nails. She acted like she didn't hear.

"You need some money?"

"Got my own," I lied. I didn't want anything from *her*.

"Oh, Billie, you make me tired. And that Godawful hair. What's wrong with you?"

The elevator door opened and I stepped in. "What's wrong with me is you," I said and watched the door slide closed, blocking out her surprised face.

I didn't even know why I'd said it. I hadn't planned to. I really didn't know if it was true or what it meant. Popped out is what it did. Ah, who cared anyway?

Elissa lived in the Village on the other side of Houston. Her building on Sullivan Street was like the Captain's, except the Rosenbergs had six rooms on the third floor. I knocked on the door.

Sylvia Rosenberg answered. "Oh, it's you," she said. Actually, this was a fairly nice greeting. Sometimes she said nothing, and other times she growled or called me a goy. A goy is someone who is not Jewish. You just never knew with Mrs. R. how it would go. "So, come in, dopey. Don't just stand there like a lox." She eyeballed my hair but said nothing.

The Rosenbergs were eating dinner. Well, at least three of them were. Sylvia never ate. Not in front of anybody. She watched. Mr. R. and Andy gave my hair the onceover.

"You want some dinner?" asked Sylvia.

I felt embarrassed dropping in just in time for chow like I'd planned it or something, and the truth was it hadn't entered my mind. So I said no thanks.

"You ate already, Billie?" goes Elissa. "That was fast."

"I skipped dinner. I wasn't hungry."

"And you're *still* not hungry?" Sylvia asked suspiciously.

"Well...I..."

"Sit already and stop pretending shyness," she said. "I hate a phony-baloney. You'll sit, you'll eat, you'll feel better."

Sometimes Sylvia could be so nice, so normal. Like a real mother.

It was a round table and I pulled up a chair between Elissa and Mr. R. Andy, the boy twin, stared at me through mean little eyes. The truth was, he was extremely handsome. But his personality took the edge off his looks. All his life he had gotten everything he wanted and it showed in his face. Spoiled rotten is what he was.

"Hello, Mr. Rosenberg," I said.

Shyly, he glanced up from his plate. "Hello," he said and looked quickly back down at his food.

"Mr. Personality," Elissa said to me out of the corner of her mouth.

The dinner was brisket of beef, farfel (like tiny macaroni pellets), and carrots. It smelled wonderful.

"You're in a pageant or something?" asked Sylvia.

"A pageant?" I said, confused.

"You're playing maybe a purple flower?"

"Oh, you mean my hair. No, no pageant."

"Then what?"

Andy said, "It's the style, Ma. Everybody's doing it."

"Who, everybody?"

"Freaks," he said, smiling in an especially mean way.

Mr. R. peeked up at me, then quickly looked back at his plate.

"Freaks?" asked Sylvia, her eyes going round.

"Shut up, Andy," goes Elissa. To Sylvia: "Never mind, Ma. I think it looks gorgeous."

Mrs. R. clucked her tongue. "Everything changes. In my day if you were a flower you were purple, not if you were a person. I'm praying no one in this house will want to be a posy so I'll have to pluck you out of our little garden here, if you get my meaning."

"Yeah, Ma," said Elissa.

Then Andy, shoveling food in his mouth, goes, "I hear your boyfriend's flown the coop."

"Still missing," said Elissa, shaking her locks.

"He's not my boyfriend," I said.

"I suppose you're wondering why I don't eat," said Sylvia, sitting down at the table. "Well, I'll tell you. Several years ago I went to visit my mother who lived at the time in Florida."

"Ma, please."

"Sylvia, you don't need to tell the girl the story," Mr. R. said.

"Don't tell me in my own house what I can say and what I can't. To continue. I went to visit my darling mama at the beach in Florida. We in turn went to visit her friend. A goy."

"That's very prejudiced," said Andy.

"What is?"

"To say a person is a goy," explained Elissa.

"But she *was.*"

"You don't need to say it. Who cares what she was? She was a person, that's all that matters. Goy or Jew, what difference does it make?" said Andy.

"A Jew would've never done what she did."

"Oh, Ma," Elissa goes.

"It's true."

Mr. R. said, "Let's change the subject."

"I like this subject. You like this subject, kid?" she asked me.

Have you ever felt like a rat in a trap? This was how I felt. Eight eyes of the Rosenbergs were upon me, six urging me to say no, I didn't like the subject and two urging me to say I did. Majority ruled. "Maybe we could talk about something else," I muttered softly.

Sylvia jumped to her feet. "You see. That is a goy for you. You feed them and they turn on you like a snake. And he says goy or Jew, what's the difference? A world, boy, a world of difference. Now get the little purple-headed goy out of here before I turn over the table."

Elissa jumped to her feet and grabbed me under the arm. "Let's split, Billie."

I managed to get a last forkful into my mouth before it was too late. In a second we were out the door and down the hall.

When we were outside on the street Elissa goes, "Boy, I got more to eat tonight than usual. How'd you do?"

"Okay. You mean she does that every night?"

"Along those lines. I guess that's why I eat so fast."

I had once criticized her for gulping down her food. I never would again.

"Sorry about that, pal."

"Hey, it's not your fault. What was the story she was going to tell?"

"It's stupid."

"Tell me anyway." I put my arm through hers. She had a tough life with Sylvia, Andy, and Herman.

"Sylvia and my grandma went to this woman's house and the woman gave her a drink. A screwdriver. And ever since then she hasn't had any appetite."

I stopped walking and looked at Elissa.

"I told you it was stupid."

"What does it even mean?"

"Who knows? You think she makes sense, Billie? My ma hasn't made sense in a long long time. You don't know how lucky you are to have a mother like yours."

"Yeah." There was no use telling her that having a mother who made sense wasn't everything. I knew what she meant and she was right. I may have had complaints about The Mother but she wasn't off the wall.

"I'm meeting Mickey," said Elissa. "But I got time. He's over at Mitch's doing some work."

At the sound of Mitch's name my heart did a loop-the-loop.

"Why don't you go over to Mitch's when Mickey leaves? You hungry? Let's have a slice, okay? I'm buying."

Amalfi's was the best pizza place in the Village, so we headed across Bleecker Street toward Seventh Avenue where it was located. "Do you think I should?" I asked.

"Huh?"

"Visit Mitch? I mean, just like that?"

"Well, here's the thing . . . I'm picking Mickey up at Mitch's place, so you could be with me and then maybe he'll ask you to stay. Anyway, at least you could explain why you didn't show this afternoon."

"True."

At Amalfi's I opened the door and felt the blast of air conditioning. Good feeling.

Elissa ordered two slices. "You want a drink?"

"Tab."

"Two Tabs," she said to the counterman. "In case you're wondering, Billie, I borrowed this money from Andy's bank."

I eyeballed her good and she knew what I was thinking.

"*Borrowed*, not stole. I'll pay it back on Friday."

The thing was that Elissa had once had a very bad habit of taking things that didn't belong to her. From Andy, her mother, her father, and stores too. It had been two years since she'd lifted anything, and I didn't want to see her start again. We had talked out the whole problem and decided we wanted to live honest lives. In everything we did. Like I said, I used to tell whopping lies. Anyway, we made a trade-off, Elissa and me. She wouldn't steal and I wouldn't lie.

We carried our slices and Tabs to a table. I took a bite of pizza and the cheese got all stringy and hung in the air. I flipped it back on the slice with my finger. "I've been thinking, maybe I should find something out about multiple sclerosis. I mean, don't you think it would be smart to know something about it?"

"Why don't you ask Mitch?"

"I don't think he wants to talk about it."

"Well," Elissa said, wiping tomato sauce from her chin, "you know what I found out. Death."

"But maybe your info was wrong. When we're finished here let's go to the bookstore."

She agreed. "The bookstore" meant only one place. On the corner of Tenth Street and Seventh Avenue was a small shop called Three Lives & Co. Three women owned and ran it. They were really neat. Jenny, Jill, and Helene.

Elissa and me, between bites of pizza and sips of Tab, went over our day and discussed again the possibilities of the whereabouts of Dino Farelli. The thing is, Elissa and me could discuss over and over and over again the same things and never get bored. There are, I've noticed, many sides to an issue. When we were done we walked up Seventh to the bookstore.

All three of the Three Lives were in the store. The thing about them was that they were all different. Jenny was the youngest and shortest and had a bubbly personality and was very talky. Jill was the oldest, had red hair and freckles, and was kind of real laid back, like they say. Helene was sort of other-worldly, but also a nature lover. She had long dark hair and sometimes she wore a baseball cap like me, and both she and Jenny wore glasses.

"Hi, Billie, Elissa," Jenny said from behind the counter, which was on a raised platform in a corner of the store. "Hey, what's with the hair?"

"I like it," said Jill.

Helene, who was also behind the counter, said, "Interesting, Billie, very interesting."

"You going punk or something?" asked Jenny, blowing out long dragonlike plumes of smoke from nose and mouth. She smoked like a maniac and everyone except Elissa was always nagging her about it but it didn't seem to do any good.

"I'm expressing myself," I said.

Helene goes, "Expression is good for the soul."

Jill smiled mysteriously.

"Gimme a break!" said Jenny.

"Listen," Elissa goes, "enough said on the

hair already. Let's get on with the business at hand."

"What business is that?" asked Helene.

"We've come to ask about a book."

"How unusual," Jill said. "What book?"

"Or books maybe," I added.

"Terrific. Hear that? Books. Plural," goes Jenny.

Helene took pity on us. "Title, please. Or titles, as the case may be."

Elissa and I looked at each other, then back at the women.

"Gimme a break! You don't know the titles, right?"

We nodded in unison.

"Subject?" asked Jill.

"Multiple sclerosis."

Their expressions changed and they all looked very serious.

"How come?" asked Helene.

"A friend has got it," Elissa said.

"Anyone we know?" Jenny asked.

"Billie's boyfriend," Elissa said.

I couldn't believe my ears.

"Dino?" asked Jill, horrified.

"Nah," said Elissa. "Mitch. Her *new* boyfriend."

"He's not really my boyfriend," I said and gave Elissa one of my best glares.

"Only a matter of time," she said.

"This guy has MS?" asked Jenny.

"He's on crutches already," Elissa answered.

Just then a few more people came into the store and Jill went to wait on them. Jenny got out the big Subject Guide book and started looking it up.

"I know we don't have anything in stock."
Helene said.

"Here's one listed," said Jenny.

"How much is it?" I asked.

"Nine ninety-five."

It was a lot of money but somehow I'd get it.
Mitch was worth a lot more to me, even at this
point when I hardly knew the guy, than a
measly ten bucks.

"Listen, Billie," Helene said, "don't worry
about the money. You can pay a dollar a week."

"Fifty cents a week," goes Jenny.

See what I mean? They were really neat.
"Thanks," I said.

"I'll put in the order tomorrow and we'll have
it next week. Come in around Wednesday. Now,
listen, are you really seriously involved with
this kid?" asked Jenny.

"He's no kid. He's an older man," said Elissa.

"Well, ex-cuse me," Jenny said.

I quickly said, "He's twenty-one and he's just
a friend, believe me."

"Just a matter of time," Elissa said again.

"Too old for you," Jill said, coming up behind
me and putting a gentle hand on my shoulder.

"And if he's sick?" Helene shrugged. "Not
that you shouldn't be nice to him and help him,
but you're asking for trouble to get involved
with somebody who . . ." She stopped talking,
shook her head.

"It's not always terminal," Jill said. "I have a
friend who's been in the remission stage for
fifteen years."

This was the first good news I'd had in days.
"No kidding? I thought it was always terminal."

The others agreed.

"Nope. The book will tell you all about it. Your friend may never get any worse than he is now."

Well, Happiness was my middle name. The truth of the matter was I'd been holding back a little on my feelings 'cause in the center of my mind was this nagging idea that Mitch was gonna die. Now I had a new slant on things and I could hardly wait to get over to Mitch's apartment.

"Thanks for everything," I said. "See you next week." I grabbed Elissa's arm and dragged her out of the store.

"Where's the fire?" she asked.

"Did you hear that? Did you? See, your info was wrong."

"Cool it, Billie. Come back down to earth. What Jill said was that it wasn't *always* terminal. That means sometimes it is."

"Well, that's a downer," I said.

She shrugged. "Sorry, pal."

Elissa was right. But at least there was hope and that still made me feel happy. "Can we go over now?"

She looked at her watch and nodded.

As we walked toward Mitch's I made a few decisions. I would try to look on the positive side of things. And I'd go slow. Stay in reality. Not get carried away. Take things the way they came. Keep it very simple.

Right.

When we crossed through the gas station to Perry Street Elissa asked, "What're you thinking?"

"Well," I answered, "I was just trying to remember how long it takes to get a marriage license in New York."

Eleven

So there I was, sitting right in Mitch's living room with him across from me, smiling. And it was nighttime, too. Almost like a date.

It had all gone very smoothly. Me and Elissa had come in and practically right away Mitch was asking me to stay. Mickey and Elissa left and I, naturally, stayed. I told Mitch all about Captain Natoli and why I hadn't showed up and he was very understanding. We put off the backgammon lesson 'cause Mitch said he wasn't much of a teacher at the end of the day. He gets tired real easily.

One thing had me worried. Either it was a new development in his disease or I just hadn't noticed it last time. When Mitch went to cross his legs, either way, he had to lift one leg over the other with his hands. I wanted to ask him about it but like I'd told Elissa, I didn't think Mitch wanted to talk about it. There was lots of stuff I wanted to ask him, not just about MS, but everything I thought of asking seemed to lead right back to the disease. I couldn't wait to get my hands on that book. Maybe it would also give advice on how to act with a person who has MS. But right now I needed some stalling time to think what to talk about next, so I excused myself and went to the bathroom.

It was right out of an ad in a magazine. He had red towels. Have you ever heard of a more wonderful color? Everything was neatly in place. I took my time inspecting everything. Not that I opened any drawers or cabinets, but I gave everything that was in plain sight a good once-over. And then I saw it! I didn't know what it was exactly, just some leather case. But the important thing about it was that in the lower right-hand corner were two gold initials: M.R. In my head I scrambled them around. Weren't they supposed to read R.M.? Why would Robert Mitchell have a leather case in his bathroom that had the initials M.R. on it? Something was screwy.

Suddenly I felt scared. Well, maybe not scared, more confused and anxious, like I was gonna have a big test in school and hadn't studied for a month. In other words, I *didn't* have all the answers.

I'd been in the bathroom long enough. I flushed the toilet to make it seem legit and went back in the living room. Mitch wasn't there but I heard him rustling around in the kitchen.

"Can I help?" I called out. Then I was scared I'd said the wrong thing.

But he answered, "As a matter of fact, you can."

His back was to me as he stood at the counter, one hand holding on to a railing the Bonus Boys had built. His crutches leaned against a closet door.

"You like Sara Lee cheesecake?" he asked, not turning around.

"Doesn't everybody?" I said. If you think I was gonna give him a lecture about sugar, I wasn't.

When he finished cutting the pieces he turned, still holding the railing with one hand and offering me my piece of cheesecake with the other. For a minute he almost seemed like an acrobat. Almost but not quite. Who am I kidding? He looked like a man who needed a railing to hold himself up. And that's the truth.

"Should we eat it here or in the living room?" he asked.

Fast as a bunny my mind made a connection. Probably it was easier for him to eat at a table. "Here," I said.

"Fine. I think I'll go to the bathroom first."

Again he swung around with one hand holding the railing and, with the other, held out his cheesecake plate for me to take. I set it on the table while he sidestepped over to his crutches. After he got them in place he took a few steps to the table, leaned down and took a bite of the cheesecake, then slowly made his way to the bathroom.

It was real painful to watch the guy. I sure didn't want to feel pity but I guess that's what I was feeling. I knew he'd hate that. But how could I help it? Weren't sorrow and pity the same thing? And what, after all, was wrong with feeling sorry that a person had MS? Should I be glad? What kind of nut case would I be if I didn't feel sorry that Mitch had MS? Mitch. Was that even his name? Again I thought of the gold-embossed letters on the leather case. M.R.

Maybe he'd changed his name! Maybe Mitchell was his *first* name, not his last. So what did the R stand for? Was it really Mitchell Robert? But *why* had he changed his name? Then again, why should I be surprised at any of this? Wasn't it all a big secret from the beginning, with Dino and Mickey creeping around and having to ask Mitch if it was okay to tell us? And hadn't Mitch said he wanted to keep a low profile? One sure way to do that was to change your name. So where was his family? What kind of mother and father would let their sick son go off and live by himself? Now I was starting to feel mad. Maybe when he got MS his family turned against him, threw him out in the cold. And then he changed his name because he wanted nothing more to do with such cruel and heartless people! What a brave man he was, my Mitch. Hey, wait a minute, Billie, where do you get this *my* Mitch stuff? Slow down.

I looked across at his plate, saw the small bite out of his piece of cake, and then got the idea. Probably if I was smart I'd keep this to myself but whoever said I was smart? The Mother said one of my big troubles was ever since I got honest and stopped telling stories, I started telling *everything*. "Billie," she said and said and said, "you don't have to tell every detail of your life to every Tom, Dick, and Harry on the street. Be selective." But that's not me. My life is an open book. I tell all. Why should I hide stuff? So this is what I did. I switched forks. Yeah, forks. After I took a bite of cake, I traded my fork for his which he'd had in his mouth. Now I put it in mine. It was practically like kissing.

Well, sort of. Anyway, it made me feel much closer to him.

I heard him coming down the hall and all of a sudden panic grabbed me round the middle like I was in a wood press in The Mother's workshop. Maybe multiple sclerosis was catching!

"Sorry I took so long," Mitch said when he came into the room.

" 'S okay." I felt numb.

He made his way over to the chair at the table, lowered himself down, then put his crutches on the floor next to him. "Try the cake yet?"

"Yes," I said weakly, "it's great."

He picked up his fork (my fork), cut a piece, and put it in his mouth. If only I'd switched back the forks when I'd thought of the contagious bit. There'd been time but now it was all too late. What was I going to do? Maybe I was still safe. I'd only put it in my mouth once. But if I had to eat my cheesecake with *his* fork, every bite, that would probably give me the disease but good. I sure couldn't tell Mitch the truth.

"Don't you want it, Billie?"

"Huh?"

"Your cheesecake."

"Oh, yeah, sure." I picked up the fork like it was a vial filled with poison, and in a way it was. Or might be. All because I wanted to be romantic and have his fork. Feh on romance. For all I knew, multiple sclerosis germs were running helter-skelter through my body even as we spoke. I cut a piece of cheesecake and millimeter by millimeter I lifted it to my lips.

And then . . . I dropped the fork. Clang onto the floor. Simple solution. I jumped up.

"Get another," he said.

"I'll wash this one."

I got some paper towel, picked up the bite of cake from the floor, threw it in the garbage, and washed the fork within an inch of its life. And when I was settled in my place again I still felt awful. Now I was safe eating my cheesecake, but there had still been the fork-in-the-mouth number. I just had to ask and hope he wouldn't hate me. Self-preservation was stronger than love, it seemed.

"Mitch? Can I ask you something about MS?"

"Yes, I guess." He studied his plate.

For sure I'd put my foot in my mouth, like they say, and I started backing off. "Maybe you'd like me not to?"

"What is it?" Now he looked up at me, his brown eyes like melted chocolate.

I thought I might faint. "Ah, nothing. Forget it." What did it matter if I caught MS as long as I could always look at that gorgeous face and into those heavenly peepers.

"Look, Billie, it's okay. It's normal to be curious about it. Probably I'd have questions of you if the situation were reversed. So shoot." He smiled and the cleft in his chin widened slightly.

I had to take him at his word. "Well, I . . . I just wondered if it's, you know, contagious?" Now I felt like that foot in the mouth was in a shoe and that shoe had cleats.

His eyes seemed to go all sad and then he shook his head from side to side. "There are a lot of misconceptions about this disease. No. It's not."

Sweet relief. "Then how do you get it?" I figured I might as well keep asking until he told me to stop.

Mitch put down his fork. "Nobody knows. Oh, there are a lot of theories, but it's really still a kind of medical mystery."

"What are the theories?"

"Well, one is that it's a virus. Another is that something goes screwy in the body and our built-in defense system, which destroys viruses, suddenly starts attacking the body's own cells. Or it might be a combination of both ideas. They just don't know." He picked up his fork and started eating again.

I didn't know if this was a signal for me to stop asking questions, but if it was I was going to ignore it. Information from Mitch about MS was better than from a book. The horse's mouth, like they say. "I know this is dumb, Mitch, but I don't know what happens. I mean, what is it, exactly?"

"Don't feel dumb, Billie. Most people don't know. Why should they? I didn't know anything about it before I got it. My family . . ."

He stopped then, looked away and a muscle started twitching in his cheek. "You finished?"

"Yes."

"Let's go back in the living room, okay?"

While he was getting up I took our plates and forks and put them in the sink. I didn't know if I should wash them or not. It was hard to know what would insult him or make him feel helpless and what was just regular. I asked myself, If he wasn't sick would I wash up for him? and the answer was no. I left the dishes in the sink.

As we walked down the short hall to the

living room I wondered if he was gonna go on telling me about MS or if that was it. I didn't think I could bring it up again. It would have to come from him.

He tried to make himself comfortable in his chair. "Tired," he said, lifting his right leg over his left.

I looked at my watch. It was a quarter to nine. "Should I go?"

"No, no. Not yet. It's just that this is a very tiring disease. And I don't sleep too well. It sort of keeps me awake. Anyway, to answer your question, I guess the simplest way to put it is that the messages from the brain don't get through right."

"But why?" I asked.

"Something called myelin, which normally insulates nerve fibers, breaks down and is replaced by scar tissue. That's what distorts the messages. Simple, huh?" He tried to smile but it just didn't work.

I wanted real bad to hold his hand or put my arm around him. Was that pity? I wondered. "How long have you had MS, Mitch?"

"Well, I got my first symptoms about a year and a half ago but nobody knew what it was. Every once in a while I'd see double and I felt very weak. My hands shook and I had this numb feeling, or more like a prickly sensation in my feet."

"What did the doctors say it was?"

He looked a little sheepish. "The truth is I didn't tell anyone for six months."

"Oh, Mitch."

"I know, I know. It was stupid. But when I finally did, it still took another three months for the doctors to diagnose it. It's a hard disease to pinpoint."

"Then what happened?" I asked.

"Then the disease kept moving like a rocket. Most people have remissions but so far I haven't had any. If I keep going like this I'll be in a wheelchair pretty soon."

He said that last like it was something to be ashamed of. "Well, lots of people get around pretty good in wheelchairs."

"Yeah, sure," he said, and I heard the bitter tinge to his words. He looked at his watch.

"I guess I'd better go."

"Sorry," he said. But he didn't sound sorry. I guessed I'd said the wrong thing.

"Listen, Mitch, I didn't mean . . ."

"It's okay. It's hard for anyone else to understand. I mean, it's easy for you to say people get around swell in wheelchairs when it's not you who's going to have to do it." He sounded mad.

"Yeah, I guess. What do I know, anyway? Sorry."

"Forget it. I know you meant well. Just don't feel sorry for me, Billie, and we'll get along great."

"No, I won't," I said, smiling. There it was again, the same request.

I told him I wouldn't be able to visit the next day because of Aunt Ruthie and the Captain, but if he wanted company that night I might be able to come over for a while. He gave me his phone number and said I should call first to see if he was up to it. Then he held out his hands and motioned me over to his chair. He took my hands in his, and in my head I heard the swell of a thousand violins. Somehow the sound of rock didn't go with this moment. I prayed my hands wouldn't sweat in his and I concentrated on not shaking. Then he said,

"I really like having you here, Billie. I think we're going to be good friends. That is, if you can put up with my moods. Sometimes I get depressed."

"That's okay. I get depressed sometimes too." The first tremble started in my knees.

"Everybody gets depressed, I guess."

"But it's different for you, huh?"

"Well, a different reason, yes. Anyway"—and now he squeezed my hands—"I like you a lot and appreciate your visits."

"Oh, I enjoy it," I said and could feel myself blushing. I prayed he wouldn't notice.

"Good," he said. And then he gave my hands a final squeeze and let go.

I don't know if I'll ever be able to explain what happened next. I guess I sort of went crazy. Well, not exactly crazy. Anyway, what I did was, I leaned down and kissed him on the cheek. You know what he did? He kissed me back on the cheek. Just like that!

I was in such a daze I hardly remember saying good-bye. Next thing I knew, I was out on the street walking home, except I didn't feel like I was walking at all. It was more like floating. The imprint of his lips still burned on my cheek. I touched my face. There was nothing there. Still, I knew it would be a long time before I washed that spot. I couldn't believe how wonderful I felt. Robert Mitchell had kissed me.

Well, so what if it was on the cheek? And so

what if I had kissed him first? Maybe he was just being polite, huh? Hadn't I done the very same thing with Captain Natoli when he'd kissed me? But it hadn't been out of politeness. It was because I wanted to. Because I cared for the Captain. And that's why Mitch had kissed me. Hadn't he?

I stopped walking. Wait a minute, what kind of a nerd was I, going on about kisses? There were more important things to think about. Things I still didn't have answers to. Like was MS terminal or not? Jill had said it wasn't but Elissa had said it was. Mitch was a better authority, for sure. But how could you ask a person if he was going to die? I'd have to wait for the book. And then I remembered another big unanswered question.

Who was M.R.?

Twelve

"Shmutzadicka!" Aunt Ruthie from the Bronx said as she stood staring at the layers of dust on Captain Natoli's furniture. That meant filthy. "Oy vay, does a person have her work designed for her." Hands on hips she shook her head in disbelief.

"You nicea young girl," the Captain said to her. Aunt Ruthie shrieked with laughter. "And you're nice yourself, Captain. Some young girl. I haven't been a young girl since ... well, who's counting? Time to get to work."

She put on an apron, which she'd brought along in a big L. L. Bean bag, tied her hair back in a red-and-yellow scarf, and rolled up the sleeves of her chartreuse blouse.

"Eliss," she said, pushing toward her a shopping cart which she'd also brought, "maybe you should do the shopping while Billie and I attack this filth. Or should it be vicey versey?"

"I'll shop," Elissa said.

"And when it's all done, the cleaning and the shopping, I'll take my two darlings for a nice cap and some of Vinnie's pie." At the mention of food her eyes lit up like two Roman candles!

"Then I can be filled up with all that's been going on in the romance department. Now let's get going."

Well, I don't mind telling you, we worked like dogs. Now what does that mean? Have you ever seen dogs work? Anyway, we knocked ourselves out cleaning every inch of the Captain's apartment. From tip to toe, from top to bottom. Sparkle was what it did when we finished.

And the cabinets were filled with soups, canned veggies, tuna, crabmeat, and of course pasta. The fridge too. Milk, eggs, cheese, fruit. Also there was meat in the freezer.

"Now, Captain, you can make yourself real meals," Aunt Ruthie said. "You know how to cook?"

"Sure thing."

The Aunt eyeballed him good. "Why don't I believe you?"

"You nicea young girl."

"Oh, brother. What do you think?" she asked us.

"I don't think he knows how to cook," I said. "Maybe he did once, but..."

"Wholeheartedly I agree. A schedule is in order. You two will have to take turns cooking for him. Morning and night. Lunch he'll manage himself."

"Okay," said Elissa, "we'll work it out."

"I'll start tomorrow morning," I said, thinking I'd be wanting to get to Mitch's in the afternoon or evening.

Elissa wasn't fooled. "You planning to always do breakfasts?" One eyebrow was cocked.

I shrugged.

"No way, José. Alternating is the only deal I'll go for."

"Yeah, sure."

"So it's settled," said Aunt Ruthie. "Superb. Now, Captain, what would you like for dinner tonight?"

"Pasta."

And pasta it was. In what seemed like minutes, Aunt Ruthie had whipped up a big tomato sauce, enough to freeze a lot of portions for the future. We stored them in plastic containers she'd brought with her. Aunt Ruthie had thought of everything.

Elissa set the Captain's small table in the kitchen and we served him his dinner of linguine and sauce. In a small bowl we put grated cheese.

He sat down to eat, Pinocchio at his feet. We watched as he took his first bite. He seemed to chew and taste for a long time, and when he looked up at us we saw that his eyes were filled with tears.

"Justa like home," he said. "Sucha nice, good young girls."

Well, nobody looked at anybody else for fear we'd bust out crying and the Captain would misunderstand. But when you've worked real hard and somebody truly appreciates it, it could make you all weepy and stuff. Anyway, we waited until the Captain finished his meal and then we walked him downstairs. He always took Pinocchio for a walk at that time. We were worried he might get lost again but he seemed pretty together, and besides, we couldn't spend every minute with him. We had to risk letting him be on his own sometimes.

After we put Aunt Ruthie's stuff back in her

car we headed toward Vinnie's but we never got there. Mickey stopped us.

"Boy, am I glad to see you guys. Hi, Aunt Ruthie."

"Hello, Mickey." Although she was polite to him, Aunt Ruthie never hid the fact that Mickey Zellan was not her favorite person. She thought Elissa could do better but admitted it was Elissa's life not hers. This was one of the ways she was different from a parent. They always thought that your life was theirs!

"What's up, Mick?" from Elissa.

"Dino's been found."

"Where?"

Mickey looked all weird then, eyes shifty. "You ain't gonna like it," he says to me.

"It's very unattractive to say ain't, Mickey," goes Aunt Ruthie.

Sometimes she *was* like a parent! I said, "Mickey, Dino's whereabouts are not really my concern so don't worry. I'm naturally glad he's been found and that's all." I was trying to sound mature.

"That's what you think," he said.

"Spit it out, Mickey," Elissa said.

"Can't we discuss this over some nourishment?" asked The Aunt.

Mickey goes, "Huh?"

"Let's have it," screamed Elissa.

"You asked for it. Okay. He's holed up with... with your old man," he said to me.

"With Ted? What do you mean?"

"They're freaked out. Nostalgia too."

"You're kidding."

Mickey shook his head, his wire-rimmed glasses practically skidding down his thin nose.

"Seems Dino went to see Ted about you and they got stoned."

"Am I hearing correctly?" from Aunt Ruthie.

"I think so," said Elissa. "What are they stoned on, Mick?"

"Not sure, but it ain't good, man."

"Well what do you want us to do?" I asked. I was burning mad. The Father was nothing but an overgrown kid. Why was I always having to take care of grown-ups?

"Somebody's gotta do somethin'." He looked desperate.

"Please," said Aunt Ruthie, "let us not stand around punching the breeze. Lead us to the scene of the crime."

So the four of us made our way over to The Father's pad. It was a gloomy little parade, I'll tell you. When we opened the door the first thing we heard was this:

"I must be validated! I must be validated!"

"What's that?" from Aunt Ruthie.

I told her it was Nostalgia screaming her brains out.

The hall was very dark and seemed miles long. Mickey led the way, Elissa next, then me, and Aunt Ruthie brought up the rear. We held hands as we tiptoed along. You could see an eerie glow at the end of the hall. When we finally emerged into the living room, we saw the light was coming from lots of candles. Nostalgia had stopped screaming and was now sitting cross-legged on a big pillow staring into space like she was seeing something horrible.

The Father, who was wearing only his underpants, seemed to be playing his clarinet, except there was nothing in his hands!

And Dino Farelli?

Dino Farelli of Bonus Boy fame, ex-boyfriend and ex-missing person, was growling and barking like a dog. His T-shirt was ripped down the back and he was on hands and knees, eyes no longer sad-looking, just crazy.

"Very nice," goes Aunt Ruthie, "extremely attractive."

And now Mickey told us the truth. "They took PCP."

"Angel dust," Aunt Ruthie yelped. She was very up on things, although I was sure she'd never laid her peepers on anything like this.

I'll tell you, if there was one thing I hated and feared it was angel dust. It was a powder produced in home labs and it was pure danger. It made people crazy. Psychotic. Kids had been known to bite off their own fingers, pull out eyes, and even kill when on dust. When Mickey and Dino had been at their worst, heavily into hash and pot, they always avoided dust. Now this. It must have been an accident. I couldn't believe The Father would deliberately give Dino dust even if he smoked it himself, which I'd never known him to do.

"How d'ya know it was dust?" asked Elissa.

Mickey looked all funny again like he wished he was miles away. "Ted told me," he said softly.

"Was it a mistake?" I asked, fingers crossed.

"Nah."

I felt a stab of pain right through my center. Why did I have to have a noodle for a father? Then shame washed over me like I'd walked into a running shower. I felt Aunt Ruthie's hand on my shoulder.

"You're not responsible for him," she goes, patting me.

"Yeah, I know," I said. And I did know. Still, in a way, he belonged to me and it made me feel bad. I knew it was different from a mother with a child but I imagined it might feel the same. But I hadn't brought old Ted up from scratch so it was something else. And even if I had, he was by this age responsible for himself . . . or should've been.

"What to do?" goes The Aunt, shaking her head. "We need to organize. This whole affair is making my hair stand on its ends. And the filth in this place. Worse than the Captain's."

"Hear that riff, man," The Father yelled, meaning the sound he was making with his nonexistent clarinet.

"Shut your mouth," said Nostalgia.

"Who are you?" Ted goes, looking at her.

Then Dino jumped up from his dog position, barked twice, growled, and looked me square in the eye. He bared his teeth and I'd never seen anything so awful-looking and scary. We all took a step or so back. The growling got louder and even though I knew it was impossible, it seemed like his teeth were growing longer. He started coming toward me.

"Behave," Aunt Ruthie said. "Behave, boy."

He answered with a loud bark.

"Anybody got a leash?" asked The Aunt.

Suddenly Dino grabbed me tight, like in a trap, his arms circling my body.

"Let go of her," from Elissa.

"Stop it, Dino," shouted Aunt Ruthie.

"Hey, man, cool it," goes Mickey.

Meanwhile, I was starting to get dizzy from Dino's grip on me.

Then all hell broke loose.

"I must be validated! At once, at once, the boundaries are melting," screamed Nostalgia.

Ted stood up. "What's happening, man? Who *are* you people?"

"It's me, Daddy," I said, pulling the old handle from my memory.

"Daddy?" goes Ted. "Daddy who?"

Dino gave me a hard squeeze and you could hear the sound of my breath coming out my mouth.

"All right, Dino," said The Aunt, "let go of Billie. Enough is plenty."

Nostalgia jumped up and grabbed Ted. "I will destroy the Evil One." She started punching him and he started punching back. It was awful.

And then Dino's hands closed around my throat. Elissa, Aunt Ruthie, and Mickey jumped him all at the same time. It was probably the shortest fight on record. The Aunt ended it with one zap to Dino's jaw.

"I hate violence," she said, "but sometimes it's the only way. Call the police, the hospital, the National Guard."

"You got a swell right hook, Aunt Ruthie," Mickey said, his estimation of her going up.

"Thanks, kid."

The Father and Nostalgia were still fighting. His nose was bleeding and her right eye was turning dark and swelling.

"Billie," The Aunt goes, "these pishers belong in a zoo but no zoo would take them. So call a hospital, please, while we do our best."

As I went for the phone I saw the three of

them trying to separate Nostalgia and Ted. While I dialed St. Vincent's I turned my back. I couldn't look anymore. There were my father and this woman trying to kill each other and my ex-boyfriend out cold on the floor. What was to see? It made me sick.

It only took about five minutes before the ambulance came. It was terrible to watch as they took the three of them away. Dino was still groggy so he didn't make a fuss. But the other two? Straitjackets and all. Have you ever seen your father put in a straitjacket? It was like having my heart crack in two.

Thirteen

The four of us sat in Vinnie's looking like we'd just come from a funeral, and I guess, in a way, we had.

"Tzotzkalla," Aunt Ruthie said to me, covering my hand with hers, "when my father was in the nursing home he started biting the nurses and doctors and anyone who got in the way of his choppers. It was not a pleasant sight to see my mild old papa chewing people out, as it were." She patted my hand.

I knew what she was trying to say. She understood how I felt about seeing The Father like that. Sometimes I thought Aunt Ruthie understood everything.

Even Mickey must have felt she was smart because he asked her, "What's gonna happen to them, huh?"

"Of this I'm not completely sure. Most likely they will all recover from their idiot dose of poison. After that, who can say?" She picked at her blueberry pie, either genuinely upset or too embarrassed to eat under the circumstances.

"I hate them," I said.

"Boy, oh boy," said Mickey, shaking his head, stringy hair swinging.

"What's that mean?" asked Elissa, dragging on a cigarette.

"It means where's her loyalty, that's what it means," goes Mickey.

"You think I should feel sorry for them or something?"

He shrugged. "Well, why not?"

"Why should I feel sorry for three dopers, huh?"

"At least Dino, man."

I couldn't believe it. Mickey was eyeballing me and sending me a clear message that somehow it was *my* fault. "Don't try to lay any guilt trips on me, Mickey."

"Well, he did it because of you."

"Tell me another," I said.

"It's true. He really loves you, Billie, but he said that you were ruining his image with that stupid purple hair."

"Oh, please," goes Aunt Ruthie, one hand up, palm out, "hold the bell. I cannot remain a silent minority when I hear such drivel. You say this boy complained of Billie ruining his image?"

"Right," from Mickey.

"But now, right now, lying in the hospital meshuga from the dust, he has a lovely image? Correct?"

Mickey said, "But it's her fault."

"This talk is giving me indigestion. In my experience, when a person does a thing that is self-destructive it is not because of another person. Maybe they use the excuse of another person, as in the case of Mr. Image loves Billie, but let me tell you, kid, it's just a fabrication."

"Yeah, well how do you know that?" Mickey asked, chin thrust out.

"I know because I've lived longer than you."

"Big deal," goes Mickey.

"Hey, shut your trap," from Elissa.

"It is a big deal," Aunt Ruthie said. "It's decades of a deal. You'll find out. The point is, putz, none of it is Billie's fault and don't try and twist. I hate twisters. Those schlemiels just don't want to face reality."

I looked down into my cap, which I'd yet to touch, and saw that the milky froth had died a sickly death. I pushed the cup away. What Aunt Ruthie said made me feel better. Even though I knew that Dino's taking drugs wasn't my fault, I still had a tiny nagging feeling that somehow it was. Hearing her lay it out the way she did made me know I was completely innocent.

Mickey was sulking, his chin in his hands. Elissa, too, looked lousy. Aunt Ruthie, on the other hand, seemed to have rallied and was devouring her blueberry pie, a light in her eyes undoubtedly caused by food intake. The thing was, I knew that at some point I'd have to go home and tell The Mother, and I sure didn't look forward to that. But it had to be done.

"Well," goes Mickey, "I'm splittin'." He stood up and eyeballed Elissa. "You wanna come?"

"Where?"

"Around."

Elissa looked at us.

"Go. Enjoy," said The Aunt.

"Yeah, go," I echoed.

"You sure?"

"Positive. Soon I must get back in my car and make my way home to Marvin."

"What about you, Billie?" Elissa asked.

I sighed. "I got to get home too." I was really going over to Mitch's, but I didn't want Mickey to know.

Elissa got up. "So you'll do breakfast for the Captain, right?"

I nodded.

"Okay. I'll see you after work tomorrow." She leaned down and kissed Aunt Ruthie. "Thanks for everything."

"My pleasure."

When they were gone Aunt Ruthie ordered herself another cap. I said I didn't want anything.

"I wish I knew what she sees in the little pisher. There is no accounting for taste when it comes to love. And speaking of love, what is going on with you and Mitch? Bring me up to date."

I did.

When I was finished Aunt Ruthie said, "I think you are right. I think the man has changed his name. Now, there could be a myriad of reasons for this. A, he could have committed a crime; B, he's ashamed of his name; C, he has a wife stashed somewhere who is trying to collect alimony. So. What do we have? From what you tell me he probably isn't a criminal. There goes A. B? Maybe. And C? Too young to have an ex-wife already, although it is not beyond possibility in this day and age. Still, I don't buy it. Poof goes C. Which leaves us nowhere. I'm some big help, huh?"

I smiled. She was a help in her way and I told her. It was just good to be able to air my feelings and my ideas. Things got creepy when you kept them to yourself.

"Another thing," I said, "I'm worried about MS being terminal."

She slapped her palm against her forehead. "Oh, boy, am I a nudnick. Well, I really cannot be blamed with all the comings and goings around here. You cannot imagine how quiet and peaceful life in the Bronx is compared."

"Why are you a nudnick?" I asked.

"Because I had this very important information for you and I forgot. A head like a grater."

"Sieve."

"Sieve, shmiv. Anyway, I went to my local library, which is right next door to Harriet Laine's Bake Shoppe. I took a small stop out to sniff at the butter cookies. They were large and . . ."

"Aunt Ruthie, please," I begged.

"Oh, yes. After the Bake Shoppe I went to the library and looked up multiple sclerosis. Guess what? It is definitely not always terminal. There is much hope for MS victims."

I couldn't believe it. My heart was singing.

"A person with multiple sclerosis can be expected to have a normal life span. In fact, Billie dear, it is unusual for a person with MS to die of it."

"Oh, Aunt Ruthie, thanks so much for telling me that."

"You are very welcome. Also, a person with MS can live a fine, productive life. It just depends on whether the person is a real person or a putz. Which is this R.M. or M.R.? Real or putz?"

"He's not a putz. But I think something funny's going on."

"I think I agree. Could you ask him about the M.R.?"

"I guess I could," I said, "but is it really any of my business?"

"True, true," she said. "So maybe you could look for more clues which aren't your business either, I realize. Nevertheless, if you are planning involvement with this fellow, it maybe is your business."

"More clues?"

"To his real identity."

"And then what?" I asked.

"And then we'll see. A step at a time, Billie. It's the only sensible way to live. Plotting and planning the future is pointless. Here today, there tomorrow, if you know what I mean."

I did, even though she'd said it wrong. What she meant was here today, *gone* tomorrow. "Okay, I'll see what clues I can come up with." Once again it was going to be Billie On The Case!

"Superb!" She finished off her cappuccino and waved to Vinnie for the check. "Now, how are you feeling about your papa?"

"I feel like hell."

"I can imagine. You have to tell your mama?"

"Yes, I think I'd better."

"Just remember not a speck of it is your fault."

I said I'd keep it up front in my mind. The check came and Aunt Ruthie paid.

"Sorry about your pop and all of them," Vinnie said.

I nodded my thanks.

Out on the corner Aunt Ruthie gave me a hug and a kiss and told me to keep in constant touch. I started toward the Village. I needed to see Mitch and then I remembered he'd wanted me to call first. I found a phone booth. It rang a long time before he answered. I told him it was me.

"I'm very tired tonight, Billie. I hope you understand."

I said I did and promised to call the next day. And I did understand but I felt bad anyway. I really had wanted to see him and talk with him. I wanted to tell him about everything that had happened.

Walking back to my loft I felt lonelier than I'd felt in a long time. I realized then that if I was going to have an involvement, like Aunt Ruthie said, I'd better get used to disappointments. Mitch was sick and no matter how I sliced it his needs and wants would probably always have to come first.

Riding up in the elevator my head was spinning. What a day. And now I had to face The Mother.

Wrong again. On the counter was a note.

Dear Billie,
I waited for you to come home but
you never did so I had to leave.
I've gone out with Tom and I
might stay overnight at his
place. Don't worry about me.
His number is 555-7989. There's
an eggplant casserole in the fridge.
See you soon.
Love,
Mom

Ruthie was right: plotting and planning the future was pointless, even if the future was five minutes ahead! You never knew what was going to come down.

In my room I lay on the bed listening to The Nightmares on my stereo. Vivian sat on my chest, her white-tipped paws curled against each other. Putnam eyeballed me and Rita kept her distance. I wondered if things could get any worse. The Father and Dino were locked up in a hospital. And so was Nostalgia. It was the first time I'd ever felt an ounce of anything for her. Mitch was not really Mitch but at least I no longer had to deal with the idea of him dying. Still, I didn't know who he really was. And, last but not least, The Mother was off with The Painter. And me? I was feeling lonely. Being alone and being lonely are two different things. I like to be alone sometimes but I hate feeling lonely. It's like drifting in space wrapped in a wet blanket and I guess that feeling prompted what I did next.

I'd never been too tight with God but now I thought maybe I'd say a prayer. It was hard to start 'cause I really didn't know how. And more than that, I didn't know what to pray for. So I hemmed and hawed around, like they say, and then finally I just said: "God, how about making everything work out the way it should?"

It was real strange how that prayer was answered.

Fourteen

Swiftly is the word for how the next two weeks went by. And a lot happened. Dino's family sent him to a rehabilitation place for drug users, The Father was back in his pad alone because Mary Beth Nostalgia Mullendorf had gone home to Minnesota, and The Mother and The Painter were tighter than Jordache jeans. This didn't bother me as much as I might've thought. Maybe it was because I was real happy how things were going with me and Mitch, or maybe it was because I kind of liked The Painter. Maybe both.

The thing I liked about The Painter was that he was a genuine grown-up. In other words, he acted his age. He had a life of some meaning. Also, he was very nice to me. And I don't mind saying that that counted for a lot.

The Mother acted different too. She was happy in another way from how she'd been. I asked her about it one day.

"True. I'm happy."

"So it takes a man to make your life fulfilled," I said, baiting her.

"Nope. It's just the last piece in the puzzle of

life. If I didn't have a sense of myself, no man could make me feel good," she said. "You have to have yourself first, and then another person enhances everything. If it's the right person. Sometimes it isn't."

I knew what she meant. Both of us had had other people in our lives before the present ones and it hadn't worked. The Father for her and Dino for me. Now she had Tom Chase and I had Robert Mitchell. I was positive he was the right person for me.

I'd seen him almost every night or afternoon (twice he'd been too tired) for the last two weeks. He'd taught me how to play backgammon and introduced me to some authors I'd never read, and sometimes we listened to music together. But most of all we talked. He told me all about his childhood and his wonderful parents and his older brother, but he didn't say anything about anyone after he'd turned twenty. It was sort of a cutoff point and I hadn't yet had nerve enough to go beyond it or ask about the initials M.R. He told me his grandfather had left him a lot of money and that he was independently wealthy and no matter how bad the MS got he'd be able to take care of himself. The main thing, he said, was that he didn't want to be a burden to anyone.

So I finally had a clue. Of sorts. I figured that Mitch had skipped out on his family because of just that. He didn't want to be dependent. Well, I'll tell you, I had a lot of wrestling to do with myself when I figured that out. See, I was beginning to realize that it was no good going it alone. The Mother needed The Painter, Captain Natoli needed me and Elissa, we needed Aunt

Ruthie, and Dino needed the rehab. So did The
Father, but he wouldn't admit it and look where
that got him? But the thing of it was that if I
could, in some crazy way, convince Mitch to go
back to his family, where would *I* be? See what I
mean? So I kept my lips buttoned. The status
quo was just great with me. I had prayed, after
all, for things to turn out the way they should
and it looked like that was happening. Why
upset the orange cart, as Aunt Ruthie would
say!

Sixteen days after our first and only kiss,
Mitch and I were rapping about Ms. No-
Talent... me. I told him how it hurt me not to
be able to do anything creative like The Mother
and The Father. Even though The Father didn't
really use his, he had it. I told Mitch that
basically I felt like a big zero. Then all of a
sudden he zonked me with a weirdo question.

"Is that really why you dyed your hair purple, Billie?"

"Huh?" I said, sounding like a nerd. But, sue
me, I didn't get the connection. "What's my
hair got to do with me having no talent?"

He smiled, two small lines like brackets around
his lips. "I used to know this guy who was
always getting into trouble doing antisocial things.
Always attracting attention to himself. Nothing
major, just enough to get noticed. I thought
maybe you wanted to be noticed, Billie."

I thought about it. I felt myself getting mad.
"I don't get it."

"Remember about three weeks ago when we
first talked about your hair, I said it was important to know the real reason we do things? I

just thought maybe the talent thing and your purple hair were connected."

Madder and madder. The thing was, he had my number and that's what was making me angry. I'd dyed my hair purple, I'd told myself, 'cause it was pretty. But the truth was it was a way of getting ATTENTION. Even if the attention was negative it was better than no attention at all.

"Billie," Mitch said, "you don't need purple hair to get noticed."

The anger had faded and now I just felt sad. "But I'm nothing. Nobody." I watched myself make a line in the rug with the side of my sandal.

"That's not true."

When I looked up at him I saw that he was shifting in his chair and trying not to show how uncomfortable he was. But I knew him pretty good by now and I could tell he wasn't feeling too hot.

"You want to rest?" I asked.

"No. I'm okay. Listen, Billie, to you being a nobody is a person who can't do something artistic, right? A nobody is somebody without a talent, yes?"

It was true. That was exactly how I felt. I nodded.

"It doesn't follow, you know."

"Easy for you to say. All you people who can do something say it doesn't matter." Mitch wrote poetry. Or had. Lately he didn't do anything much.

"Look, I'm no real poet or I'd be writing."

"You've won prizes and you'll write again but I can't even rhyme June and moon."

"So what?" he said.

"And I can't draw and I'm tone-deaf and I'd rather be dead than go on a stage and..."

"But you know how to love."

I looked at him, not getting what he meant. "Doesn't everybody?"

"You kidding?" Slowly he shook his head from side to side. "Knowing how to love, how to give to other people, is the best talent of all. And not many people have it. You do. You're lucky. And so is everybody who knows you."

I knew my cheeks were burning red. Taking compliments wasn't my strong suit.

Mitch went on. "Look how much you've given the Captain. Not too many people your age would bother with an old man like that."

"What else could I do?"

"You could have ignored the whole thing. Plenty of others would have. His own family did."

"The Captain's a sweet old man," I said.

"To his family he was obviously a pain. See, that's what I mean about you. And take me, for instance."

"You?"

"Sure. Look at all the time you've spent with me. And what do you get in return?"

He had to be kidding! Didn't he know? I couldn't let him think spending time with him was some kind of sacrifice on my part, so I blurted out: "I love you, Mitch."

"And I love you," he said, real easy like.

Well, you could've knocked me over with a piece of pizza. I couldn't believe it. I'd hoped, but never really thought, he'd feel the same way. "You really do?" I asked.

"Sure I do. Anyway, the point is, your talent is giving. Loving."

I wasn't too nuts about how he'd sloughed off the part about loving me, but right now I was trying to zero in on this talent rap. I said, "Loving seems pretty easy to do."

"That's because it's natural for you."

"So you think I shouldn't've dyed my hair, huh?"

"I didn't say that. It's your hair."

"You like it or hate it?" I asked.

"It's a pretty color. What's the natural color?"

"Boring brown."

"But it's yours. And I bet it isn't boring. Nothing about you could be boring. You don't need purple hair to be noticed. Your personality makes you very visible, Billie."

These were very loving words and they meant a whole lot to me. But they were just *words*. When Dino and me had said we loved each other, we'd done a lot of heavy-duty kissing. But this was as if we'd told each other we liked salami or something. It was all very weird.

"You understand what I'm telling you?" Mitch asked.

I told him I did which was true. I wanted very much to stay and talk more about our love for each other and everything else, but it was my night to make supper for the Captain. "I have to go," I said.

"See what I mean? You'd rather stay and talk, wouldn't you? And yet you're off to make an old man's dinner."

"That's my job."

He smiled. "Come here," he said, motioning me over to him.

My heart *ka-boom*ed in my chest and I was
sure he could hear it. "Must be thunder," I
said.

"Didn't hear anything."

I was standing right next to his chair wondering how we were going to manage this. Should
I kneel? Sit on his lap? What? There was a
burning feeling right below my ribs like someone had lit a match in there. And sweat, for a
change, started pouring down my sides. Then
he held up his arms and I knew I was just
supposed to lean over. I directed my lips at his,
and in my ears was movie music, loud and
clear. My eyes were closed and then they popped
open as if I'd been slapped. The kiss was on my
cheek, my lips hanging in the air like two fools.

"You're wonderful," Mitch said and he
squeezed my arm.

"You too," I mumbled. "I'll see you tomorrow."

I got out of there pronto. Suddenly, Confu-
sion was my middle name. The guy had said he
loved me and that he thought I was wonderful
so what was wrong with that? Why wasn't
anything ever good enough for me? I crossed
Seventh Avenue, passed Three Lives bookshop,
and turned down Tenth Street. The book I'd
gotten on MS was helpful but it didn't say word
one about the love stuff except to say a person
with MS could get married and lead a long and
normal life in that department. So Mitch's pla-
tonic kiss probably had more to do with the fact
that he was an older man and a poet. Sure!
That was it. He didn't need to maul me like
Dino had tried to sometimes. Mitch was romantic and sensitive and knew how to go about
these things. Who needed a lot of dumb mak-

ing out to prove you were in love? Not this cookie! Me and Mitch, we were above that. That was for kids. The important thing was how we *felt*, not what we did. How *I* felt was in love. And I knew he felt the same way. He'd said it to me, hadn't he? I heard his words again: "And I love you." Proof positive. It *was* like a movie. An old one like they have on television. You never saw a lot of physical stuff in those movies when the boy and girl said they loved each other. Everything was understood. I guessed maybe Mitch was old-fashioned.

As I turned down Thompson Street toward the Captain's, I was feeling really high. There was nothing more fulfilling than loving and being loved. The Mother was right: it was the final piece in the puzzle of life.

Before I started up the stairs I wiped my face with my red handkerchief I carried in my pocket. Hot was not the word for the day. I took a breath and started climbing. When I got to the sixth floor I was like a piece of cooked spaghetti. I practically crawled down the hall. After I rapped twice and got no reply, I let myself in with my key. I'd start dinner and the Captain, for sure, would be back by the time it was ready.

When the door swung open and I saw the Captain and Pinocchio in the chair I got a bit of a surprise. Pinocchio was deaf so that's why he hadn't barked when I knocked. And the Captain was asleep. I tiptoed past them into the kitchen. Broiled chicken breasts, new potatoes, and steamed carrots were on the menu for that night. Me and Elissa made out the menus at the beginning of each week. It was easier that way.

Everyone in the neighborhood said they'd
never seen Captain Natoli looking so good.
And Caroline, the butcher, always gave us extra
weight when she knew we were shopping for
him. The grocer too added an extra bean here
and an extra carrot there. Captain Natoli was
practically an institution in our neighborhood. I
popped the chicken into the broiler and washed
the potatoes. When that was done I scraped the
carrots, sliced them up, and put them into the
little steamer we'd bought. Then I decided to
wake up the Captain.

Pinocchio was yawning as I came into the
room, his open mouth like a black pit. I walked
over to the Captain and reached out to touch
him. Pinocchio gave a ferocious growl and I
jumped back.

"Hey, what's wrong, boy?" Real careful like I
put out my hand. And again he growled, showing his motley gums.

Since he had no teeth there wasn't too much
to be afraid of but the whole thing was creepy.
Why should he act like that? Well, anyway, I
reached past him and the little dog clamped his
toothless mouth around my wrist. But even
though I'd instinctively pulled back I'd touched
Captain Natoli's arm. He hadn't moved.

I was starting to get a sinking feeling, like the
bottom of my stomach was leaking. "Pinocchio,"
I said, "be a good boy."

He answered with a *grrrrr.*

"Captain Natoli," I called. "Hey, Captain it's
a nice young girl here."

No answer. No movement. I think I knew
then but I couldn't face it. I forced myself to
really look at the Captain. The color of his skin

had changed from its usual rosy brown to a whitish gray. I stared at his chest. There was no sign of breathing. At least I couldn't see any. "Captain Natoli," I said, trying to make myself calm, "can you hear me?"

There was no answer, only the sound of Pinocchio's wheezy breathing. The dog watched me like he was guarding a treasure and, sure enough, he was.

I was pretty certain that the Captain was dead but I'd read of people who seemed dead and weren't, so I wasn't about to make any heavy pronouncements myself. I needed help.

I ran real fast out of the apartment, down the steps, and up the blocks to Vinnie's. Elissa was too far away and Vinnie was the only person I could think of. The place was crowded with dinner customers and Vinnie was real busy cooking but I didn't care. I went behind the counter and told him what I thought had happened.

"You sure?" he asked, face going pale.

"No. That's why I need you."

"You want I should come with you, huh?"

"Please."

"Okay." He gave some orders to his employees and came around the counter, still wearing his big white apron over his stained T-shirt. Together we jogged across Prince and down Thompson. Then we made our way up the stairs to the Captain's.

Vinnie, not being in the best of shape, was all out of breath when we went inside. Pinocchio was still on guard, sitting on the Captain's lap. I'd prayed that the Captain would be awake now, eyes shining, smiling his smile. But, of course, he was just as I'd left him.

"Jeez," Vinnie said, standing over Captain Natoli.

"What d'ya think?"

Sweat ran down Vinnie's face and he looked caved in. He shook his head back and forth real slow. "I think so."

Pinocchio growled as Vinnie reached out a hand.

"He's got no teeth," I said.

"Yeah, I know." He lifted up the dog who kept on growling and trying to bite him. "Where's the bathroom?"

I showed him and he put Pinocchio inside and shut the door. It was awful because the poor old dog kept whining and crying. Vinnie went back to the Captain then and reached out a shaking hand to try to find a pulse in the old man's throat. Next he felt the Captain's wrist.

"He's gone," he said. "Well, he probably didn't suffer none."

"I can't believe it," I said.

Vinnie looked at me and put his big arm around my shoulders. "Ah, hell, kid, you done real good by this old man."

Even though I felt like I'd been punched in the stomach I couldn't cry. I guess I was saving it for later. I went into the kitchen and turned off everything that was cooking. When I came back into the living room I said, "What should we do now?"

Vinnie was wiping his eyes when he answered. "You go home. I'll take care of everything. He got a phone?"

I told him no. "What about Pinocchio? I'd take him but I've got three cats."

"Don't worry none. I'll take care of him too." He went to the bathroom door and opened it.

Pinocchio ran out as fast as his stiff old legs would carry him, and with a squeal of pain he jumped to the Captain's lap, turned around to face us, and started growling.

"Boy, oh boy," said Vinnie, "that's love for ya. Well, I guess he can stay for now. I'll get him later."

When Vinnie left me at the corner I practically ran home. Funny thing was, when I got there I didn't cry at all. No one was home except the cats, and the first thing I did was go in my bathroom and strip the purple color from my hair. It took a long time and when I was done my hair was completely white. I didn't have any brown dye to put it back to its natural color, so it would have to stay white like that until the next day. I don't know what made me do that except somehow it seemed the right thing. Captain Natoli was dead and for some reason having purple hair seemed disrespectful or something. And I guess what Mitch had said to me had sunk in somewhere. I didn't need it anymore and this was a perfect time to get rid of it. My hair had grown more than an inch, and it stood straight up like a long crew cut. So being white, it was like I'd had a shock or something!

As I was walking to my bedroom, I realized I hadn't told Elissa about the Captain. I stopped still in my tracks. I'd have to go out and find her 'cause it was my responsibility to tell her. But it was the last thing I wanted to do. I didn't want to go out and I didn't want to say those words. All of a sudden life felt very hard. Still, no tears would come. I wanted to cry 'cause inside my chest there was what felt like a hard ball the size of a grapefruit. Maybe if I cried the grapefruit would disintegrate. I squeezed shut my eyes. Nothing. Oh, well, all I could do then was go find my pal.

I put on my blue baseball cap and pushed the elevator button. When the door opened The Mother was there.

"Hi, Billie," she said, all smiles. Then, "Hey, what's wrong?"

"What d'ya mean?" I could never believe that she noticed anything about me.

"You look awful. Are you sick?"

She reached out to touch my cheek and I pulled away.

"Sorry," she said sarcastically.

Now why did I do that? It hurt her real bad, I could see.

She asked me if I was going out. I told her I was and she said to be back early and then she noticed the white ends of my hair sticking out from my cap.

"Oh, no. What'd you do to your hair now?"

"I took out the purple and tomorrow I'm putting back my real color."

Her eyes brightened. "Oh, well, great. I think that's a terrific decision. What made you . . ."

"Captain Natoli's dead," I burst out.

We stood there quiet for a few seconds and then she asked me what had happened. I told her everything, my words coming out like they were doing somersaults. When I was finished she said:

"Oh, Billie, why didn't you come and get me?"

"Get *you*? Why?"

"Because I'm your mother. I mean, you needed help and I would have helped you."

"I never thought of you," I said. It was true, but when I said the words, The Mother's eyes filled with tears and so did mine.

"Billie," she said softly, "I'm so sorry."

"For what?"

Tears, two of them, ran down her cheeks. "You never thought of me. That's my fault. I guess I haven't been very present."

I shrugged.

"Forgive me?" she said and held out her arms.

You better believe it, I fell into those arms like they were two...two arms of a mother! And then we both started bawling. We held each other tight and cried and cried. It was some waterworks display, I'll tell you.

She kissed my face and said, "I'm very sorry about Captain Natoli. Is there anything I can do?"

I started to say no and then I realized there was. "I have to tell Elissa."

"You want me to go with you?"

I nodded.

"Let's go," she said.

In the elevator we held hands and even though I felt wrung out and very sad about the Captain's death, there was a part of me that seemed more together than it had been in a long time. It was neat to have The Mother on my side.

Fifteen

It was the first Monday in August, two weeks since the Captain had died. I hadn't seen Mitch for three days 'cause me, The Mother, The Painter, and Elissa had gone to the beach for a minivacation. We'd had a really neat time. The weather had been great, the ocean salty and warm, and we'd all had a lot of fun. Still, I'd missed Mitch a whole lot. During the days after the Captain's death Mitch had been a wonderful comfort to me. Just the way I'd excluded The Mother from my thoughts when I needed help and love, I'd excluded Mitch too. When I'd left Vinnie the night the Captain died, it never dawned on me I could go to Mitch for sympathy. I just X'ed him out 'cause of his condition. That had been a real injustice.

He asked me when I saw him next why I hadn't come right over to him, and when I didn't answer he got mad first and hurt second. In the days after that I learned that just because a person has a disability doesn't mean he can't give love and comfort. In a way I had chalked him off as less than a human being, and that was a terrible thing to do.

A few days after Captain Natoli died so did Pinocchio. Vinnie had taken him home with him. He told me the old dog died in his sleep just like the Captain had. That had started me up all over again. Mitch had been real kind and encouraged me to cry and cry until there were no tears left.

With the Captain gone there was a hole in my life but I filled it up with seeing more of Mitch. He'd given me a key, and when I opened the door after those three days away I got a terrible shock. Mitch was sitting in the living room in a wheelchair.

"What happened?"

"It's been coming for a while now. I just didn't tell you."

"Well, why didn't you?" I asked.

"I guess I didn't want to face the truth. The doctor came on Saturday morning. I just can't make it on crutches anymore. It's all over."

"Nothing's over," I yelled.

"Don't be a dope."

"Mitch, please. Don't give up." I knew from the reading I'd done that just because he'd gotten to this stage didn't mean he was gonna die or that he couldn't go on functioning. If he wanted to.

"You don't understand," he said.

"Yes, I do."

"Now I'll never go out again," he said bitterly.

"Oh, Mitch." The truth was he never went out anyway. A few times I'd suggested we go out for a walk, but he always made excuses and said we'd do it "tomorrow." But tomorrow never came.

He read my mind. "I was going to go out this week."

"Yeah, sure."

"Let's skip it, okay? Would you do me a favor?"

I was always glad to do stuff for him, 'cause he made it hard to give him much help. Pride was a killer, I was learning.

"I need a handkerchief and as long as you're here . . . in my top drawer, right-hand side. It's one thing the Bonus Boys and I didn't think of."

"What's that?"

"The chest of drawers is too high for somebody in a chair."

"We can go shopping for a lower chest," I said.

His face flushed and his eyes got narrow. "Damn it, Billie, don't be so stupid. I can't go shopping."

I turned away from him then 'cause I didn't want him to see the expression on my face. I was mad that he was being such a quitter and hurt that he'd called me stupid. "I'll get your handkerchief," I said.

I'd never been in Mitch's bedroom before. Even though it was small and compact there was enough room for the wheelchair. And except for the chest of drawers I saw that he'd be able to manage okay. I started across the room to get the handkerchief when I saw it. On his night table was a picture of a woman. She had long blond hair that curled under at the ends, big eyes, a small nose, small mouth; her face was sort of shaped like a heart. I got closer to the photo and I saw the writing at the corner. It said: "All my love, Sarah."

Have you ever felt like it was the end of the world? Like a lot of bricks were crashing and tumbling around you and the floor you were standing on was opening up and underneath was a cavern so dark and huge and never-ending it was as if you were as big as the head of a pin? That's how I felt at that moment.

I had never mentioned any love stuff to Mitch again, telling myself we were too mature for that kind of talk. And after spending time with him I'd find a way to interpret things he'd said to mean he was in love with me. Don't get me wrong. I didn't know I was playing games when it was happening, but in this instant, while I stared at The Blonde's picture, it all clicked into place. I'd been snowing myself. Mitchell Roberts, or whatever his name was, wasn't any more in love with me than Vinnie was! Sure, he loved me. Like a friend. And if he was in love with anyone it was The Blonde. Sarah.

I don't know what made me do it but I picked up the picture and turned it around. On the back of the frame it was stamped: "Crawford Photographers, 106 Old Bachman Rd., Greenwich, Connecticut." I zapped the info onto my brain, not knowing why. Quickly, I got the handkerchief, and feeling like somebody had pulled the plug and let my heart out, I went back to the living room.

When Mitch took the handkerchief from me, he said, "I'm sorry I snapped at you, Billie."

"Ah, don't sweat it," I said. I very much wanted to ask him about Sarah. I'd never stepped over the unspoken rule of what or who we could talk about, but this was getting to be more than I could handle.

"Why are you looking at me like that?" he asked.

"Like what?"

"Like, I don't know...like something's up."

I took a deep breath. "Something *is* up."

"What?"

The thing I wanted to say was: How about telling me the truth for once? Where's your family? Who's Sarah and why did you change your name? Guess what? I couldn't. Instead I said, "Let's go out."

"Very funny."

"I'm not being funny. You said you were planning to go out this week, so now's as good a time as any, as far as I can see."

"Well, that was before. I'm not going out in this thing." He slammed his hands down on the arms of the wheelchair.

"Why not?"

"Maybe you ought to leave," he said.

Nothing like this had ever happened between us before.

"I mean it," he said. "You just don't understand what it's like."

I figured I had nothing to lose so I said, "I understand plenty. I happen to know that Robert Mitchell isn't your name and that you dumped your family and your girl."

His mouth dropped open. "How do you know that?"

Part of me had hoped I was wrong. But his reaction told me I was right. "I just know."

"Well, so what?"

"So, why'd you do it? Why'd you run away?"

I held my breath, not knowing if he'd answer or order me out.

"Because I didn't want their damn sympathy. And I don't want yours either."

"I'm not giving you any," I said.

"I think you'd better go."

"Glad to," I said, "but before I do I wanna tell you, Mitch, I think you're an egomaniac."

You would've thought I'd slapped him across the face. Now that I'd started I couldn't stop. "You're the most selfish person I know. You tell me all about my talent for giving, well, what about you, huh? When are you gonna give?"

He didn't answer, just pressed his lips together and stared at me hard.

I went on. "How do you suppose your parents and Sarah feel? Do they know where you are?"

I was surprised he answered but he did by shaking his head no.

"That stinks," I said. "They must be out of their heads with worry over you."

"Listen, Billie, you don't know what it was like. All they wanted to do was fuss over me and make me a baby. And Sarah...Sarah wanted to marry me."

I thought I might faint. "What's wrong with that?" I forced myself to say.

"You have to be kidding. Marry a cripple?"

If Sarah loved him and wanted to marry him, who was he to say no? I told him that and asked him the all-important question: "Do you love Sarah?"

"I did."

"And now?"

"I don't have the right to love anyone," he said.

That included me. "That's bull."

"What do you know? You're just a kid."

I guess he could've said almost anything but that. He'd always treated me like a peer and now the truth came out. I was just a child to him. "I may be a kid, Mitch, but I'm not a coward."

"What's that mean?"

"It means *you* are. You're a quitter and a coward. Only cowards run." How could I ever have thought he was brave to want to be alone?

"What's cowardly about doing something for myself? Being independent?" Sweat dotted his forehead like tiny seeds.

"There's being independent and there's being stupid, stubborn, and selfish," I said. "Who the hell do you think you are, anyway?"

Puzzled, he asked me with his eyes what I meant.

"You think you're God or something? Everybody needs other people. Who are you to think you can go it alone?"

"I don't want sympathy."

"Oh turn off that old song, it's flat. You're just trying to be some kind of big shot and all you're doing is hurting people."

"Please go," he said.

This time I listened. Just as I got to the door he called my name, and when I turned around I prayed he was going to ask me for help. But he didn't.

What he said was, "You'd better leave the keys."

It was like a kick in the pants. "Yeah, sure." I

took the keys from the pocket of my overalls and placed them on a little stand near the door. "So long, you gutless wonder," I said and slammed out.

So that, like they say, was that. The love of my life had kicked me out. And not only that, he'd never ever been in love with me. I was a kid to him. The truth had been eyeballing me all along but per usual, I hadn't wanted to see it. Instead, I'd pretended when he'd said he loved me that it meant more than it did. Somewhere I'd known the truth but I couldn't face it 'cause it wasn't how I wanted things to be. And now it was feeling worse than if I'd faced it right in the beginning.

Love and truth were crazy things. I kept wishing I hadn't said all that stuff to Mitch but I'd meant everything I'd said. I knew it had hurt him and I also knew I'd said it 'cause I loved him. And he loved The Blonde.

That made me remember some dumb old movie I'd seen on television. When the man lost the woman he said, "If *I* can't have you, nobody can," and then he shot her. That was just how I was feeling. Not that I was going to shoot him but I sure didn't want that Sarah to be with him.

I found myself at The Owl and went inside, where I knew I'd find Elissa and Mickey. They were in the back playing a game of pinball. Elissa, I was happy to see, was beating him.

"Hiya, pal," said Elissa.

"Hot news flash," goes Mickey.

"Yeah, what?"

"Dino's gettin' out next week."

"Good for Dino," I said. I really was happy for him but I had no desire to see him.

"Boy, you're really a friend," said Mickey.

"Can it," said Elissa. "What's up, Billie? You look lousy."

"Finish your game first," I said.

The lights flashed and the sounds beeped, and when they were done she'd beaten him by two hundred thousand points. Mickey sulked and went to get a Coke.

"Okay, let's have it," said Elissa.

I told her everything. What he said and what I said.

When I was done she said, "You were pretty rough on the guy, don'tcha think?"

"What guy?" asked Mickey, coming back with a Coke for each of us.

"Thanks," I said. So it was sugar. So what? At a time like this, who cared? I didn't want to tell Mickey about what had happened with Mitch, and Elissa knew it.

"Just somebody you don't know, Mick. Why don'tcha play with Rudy over there? Me and Billie need to talk."

"Yeah, okay," said Mickey.

We sat at a table and Elissa lit a cigarette. "Are ya gonna call him and apologize?"

"For what?"

"For what you said, Billie."

"But I meant it. He *is* a coward."

"Billie . . ."

"I know what you're thinking," I said. "He's sick, yes, but that doesn't mean his life has to be over or that he has to cut everybody out of it who loves him."

"He hadn't cut you out until you got all crazy, yelling at him and..."

I put up my hand, signaling her to stop talking so I could think. It was true. How come he'd let *me* hang around and get him things and be nice to him and love him? The answer was simple when I let myself look. I wasn't family and I wasn't Sarah. In other words, folks, I just wasn't that special. That news went down hard. I told Elissa what I'd just thought.

"But that doesn't mean 'cause you weren't number one that you were number four thousand, know what I mean?"

"No," I answered.

"I mean, one thing doesn't cancel out the others. Mitch really likes you. He even told you he loved you. That's something, Billie."

"Yeah, something."

"It's a lot," she said.

She was right. I was doing okay. The thing of it was I needed to look this problem square in the eye. Mitch was my *friend*, no more, no less. Even though he'd thrown me out he was still my friend. Sarah was his lover, not me. And I had a choice. I could keep him to myself or give him back to Sarah.

It would be easy to keep him to myself. I'd go back to his apartment, tell him I was sorry, and pick up where we'd left off. I'd never mention The Blonde or his family or going out in his wheelchair. And then what? Then I could start pretending again and what would I really have? But more than that, what would Mitch have? He'd have a friend who was sixteen years old and who in a few weeks was going back to high school and in another year was going off to college. I could have him to myself now but what about later? Mitch had said I was giving and loving but this thinking sure didn't seem either one. Selfish was becoming my middle name. Whether he knew it or not, or liked it or not, Mitch needed someone who could give him more than I could. And someone he loved more than like a sister. In other words, he needed The Blonde. Feh!

"What are you thinking, Billie?" Elissa asked.

"I'm thinking we gotta go to Greenwich, Connecticut."

"Huh?"

"And I'm thinking we need somebody with a car."

"You mean...?"

"Yup."

"I'll phone her."

When I got through explaining the whole thing to Aunt Ruthie from the Bronx, I asked her if she'd drive us to Greenwich on Saturday. And then I asked her if she thought that trying to find Sarah was meddling.

She said, "You wish my expert and honest opinion?"

"Yes," I said.

"Absolutely this is terrible meddling. I'll see you Saturday at noon."

Sixteen

Raindrops were falling on our heads. Well, not exactly on our heads. They were dropping on the roof of the car me, Elissa, and The Aunt were riding in. We were on the Merritt Parkway heading toward Greenwich, Connecticut. I don't mind saying I've felt better in my life. It was like I was uncomfortable inside my skin. Everything itched and my glasses kept sliding down my nose. At least it was cool in the car with the air conditioning going but it didn't help with the smoke from Elissa's cigarettes. I waved my hand around trying to show her how much the smoke bothered me.

"Very subtle," she goes.

"So take the hint."

The Aunt said, "When are you going to get rid of that lousy habit, kid?"

"No nagging, please," said Elissa.

"Your life," said Aunt Ruthie. "You never smoked, Billie?"

"I tried it and hated it. It doesn't make sense to me. I can't understand why people would want to put smoke in their mouths."

"Can it," said Elissa.

"The exit is coming up," I said, feeling really nervous now. What if we were making a terrible mistake? The thing was, I was still torn. I wanted to find the mysterious Sarah and I didn't. We swung off the parkway.

"What I'm thinking," goes The Aunt, "is we find a gas station and ask for directions to the street. Best, yes?"

"Yeah." What I wanted to do was tell her to turn around and head home. But I kept my lips zipped.

A few minutes later we were pulling out of a gas station with the directions to Old Bachman Road. I knew that if we tracked down The Blonde, got her name and address, it'd be too late to do anything then except go ahead. There'd be no turning back after that point. We stopped at a light. "I can't go on," I yelled.

"What's wrong?" asked The Aunt. "You're sick, maybe?"

"Cold feet," said Elissa.

"I'll turn down the air conditioning," Aunt Ruthie said.

"She's chicken," Elissa explained.

"Please, let me pull over and we'll discuss."

When the light changed Aunt Ruthie maneuvered the big car over to the curb. My head was hanging down, chin to chest. I couldn't remember when I'd felt worse. Maybe when the Captain died but that was different, although in some ways this felt like a death too.

"So, Billie, spill the peas."

"Beans," I said softly.

"Beans, shmeens, tell," said The Aunt. She patted my hand. It was like words were jumbling through my brain, smacking against each other and crashing in my ears.

"I don't mean to appear too smart for my own good, but I think I know what's wrong," goes Elissa.

"So somebody tell already," Aunt Ruthie said.

"If we find the Sarah woman, maybe she'll take Mitch back here with her, and then where will Billie be in terms of Mitch?"

"Ah, I see. Is that it, Billie?"

I nodded.

"Hmmmm," went The Aunt, "that is a problem. Still, all problems have solutions. Suppose we go home now, just forget Old Bachman Road and the Sarah woman. We pretend we never heard of a photographer named Crawford. You make up with Mitch and then what?"

"I dunno. I guess we go on like we were."

"And all the time you're going on, you know there's a woman in Greenwich who's wondering where her loved one is and how he's doing."

"Start the car," I said.

"Where to?"

"Old Bachman Road."

"You see," Aunt Ruthie said, "every problem has a solution. I'm proud you are not going to sink to the occasion, Billie."

The Aunt was exceedingly smart. I hadn't really understood it, but from the moment I saw that address on the back of the picture, the jig was up. My wavering back and forth wasn't an act or anything dumb like that 'cause in my conscious brain I was in conflict. But deep down I guess I'd always known from that moment what I was going to do. It was still a puzzle, though, why I'd turned that picture over. I wondered if it had been one of the answers to my prayer that everything should turn out the way it was supposed to. You never knew about things like that.

All of a sudden we were pulling up in front of a group of stores.

"One-oh-six Old Bachman," said The Aunt, like an announcer. "I say we all go together."

I was glad of that 'cause I never could've done it alone. Inside 106 we found ourselves in a kind of waiting room. A man with a flat nose and round eyes sat behind a desk.

Aunt Ruthie eyeballed him good, took a deep breath, and said, "Are you the photographer?"

"No, madam, obviously not."

"So what's obvious?"

"Do I look like a photographer?"

"Well, I don't know what a photographer looks like," she goes.

Flat Nose sighed. "What is it you wish, madam?"

"I'm not a madam," she said. "So, is the photographer in?"

"Would you like to make an appointment?" He licked his lips. "Is it your children you wish to have photographed?"

"I want to speak to the photographer. Crawford, I believe, is the name."

Elissa broke in. "We don't want an appointment. We want to talk, that's all."

The man narrowed his round eyes into slits. "What *is* this?"

"This," goes The Aunt, "is a delegation to speak to Mr. Crawford about something very private and not for the ears of an employee.

And don't bother saying another word, buster. Call the boss or you're in big trouble."

The man's mouth twitched and jumped and then he got up. "Just a minute, please." He went into a back room.

The Aunt said, "You start nice, and if they don't respond to humanness, you get tough. A simple everyday rule."

We smiled at her, feeling very proud to be in her company. In a minute Flat Nose came back and told us to go into the room he'd just come out of.

"Thank you very kindly," said Aunt Ruthie.

"My pleasure," the man said, looking daggers at her.

The back room was a big studio-type place with huge standing lights and lots of props sitting around, like potted plants, wicker chairs, sculptures, and lots of different-colored drapes hanging all over. And Mr. Crawford was Ms. Crawford!

"Oh, boy, am I a chauvinist piggie," said Aunt Ruthie. "Right away I assumed it was a man."

And so had I but I didn't say so. Funny how old ideas hang on.

The Crawford woman stood up. She was real tall, maybe six feet, and her red hair stuck out in little curls all over. "May I be of some service?" she asked in a nice voice.

"Yes you may," said The Aunt. "We, my niece and my friend here, are trying to locate a particular individual because of a matter of life and death, and we thought you might know where we can find her."

I realized I'd been like a mute all through this

and it was time I got into it. "We're looking for Sarah," I said.

"Sarah who?" asked Ms. Crawford.

"I don't know her last name," I said.

The Crawford woman's eyebrows made two arches.

"Allow me to explain, please," said Aunt Ruthie. And she did. When she was finished we all three waited for The Photographer's answer.

Finally she said, "I see," and then she walked to a big filing cabinet, went searching around, pulled out something, and came back to us. She held out a picture . . . *the* picture. "Is this the young woman you mean?"

"That's her," I yelled.

"Sarah Roberts is her name. And I think the young man you're referring to is . . . was her fiancé, Mitchell Redfern. He disappeared from here about four months ago."

M.R. and Sarah Roberts. He'd taken her name. I was sure now that he still loved her. But we'd have to find out if she still loved him.

Ms. Crawford went on. "Everyone has been very concerned about Mitchell. I'm glad to hear he's . . . Well, to be perfectly honest, his family thought he might have killed himself."

I felt sick just thinking about it. But I knew that the way Mitch was headed, in time it might not be such a farfetched idea.

"Will you give me the address of Sarah Roberts?" said The Aunt.

The Redhead thought for a couple of seconds, which seemed like hours, then said, "Yes, yes of course," and her face cracked a real, genuine smile. Looked good.

In less than fifteen minutes we were pulling up outside of the biggest house I'd ever seen other than in the movies. It was a stone-type joint and the driveway leading from the street was very, very long. There were big trees and bushes and flowers all over the place.

"A far cry from the Bronx," said Aunt Ruthie.

"Or Sullivan Street," goes Elissa.

"Or Prince," I added.

"Me," said The Aunt, "I'd go nuts here. Wide-open spaces, rolling lawns, and birds chirping give me the goose lumps. So let's get this show on the stage." She opened her door and we followed.

There was no turning back now. This was it. If Sarah Roberts still loved Mitchell Redfern, it was all over for you-know-who. As we walked up the wide steps to the door, a little part of me hoped that Sarah had fallen for some other guy by now or, better yet, had moved to Africa!

"Do not be intimidated no matter what," said Aunt Ruthie. "The only difference between us and these people is about four million dollars and all that is is a lot of paper. Looking at it this way may give you confidence." She reached out to ring the big brass bell and I noticed her hand was trembling slightly. More and more I was seeing that even grown-ups didn't have it all together all of the time. I used to think when you got to a certain age nothing got to you, that you just sailed through things, but I had that one all wrong.

There was a little wait before the big carved wooden door opened. A balding man wearing a dark suit and tie said, "May I help you?"

Aunt Ruthie introduced herself and said she

wished to see Sarah. Baldy asked us to come in and wait. We stood in the middle of a big hall which was more like a room. Leading down into this hall was a circular staircase with a long wooden banister. It must've been great for Sarah to slide down when she was a kid.

In a minute or two Baldy came back and asked us to follow him into the library. Well, I gotta say, outside the New York Public, I never saw so many books. There was even a ladder so you could get to the upper shelves.

"A good sign," said Aunt Ruthie. "Large readers."

"Maybe it's for show," Elissa said.

"This is possible. I have heard of such things."

The big double doors opened and a woman about the age of Aunt Ruthie, fortyish, but who looked very different, wearing a pink linen dress, a string of pearls, stockings, and brown-and-white shoes with little heels, entered the library. Aunt Ruthie, by the way, was wearing her red cotton slacks, with matching blouse and yellow espadrilles. Hanging from her ears were silver bells that tinkled when she moved her head. Before the woman could say anything, Aunt Ruthie introduced herself and said we'd come to see Sarah.

I guess suspicious was the best word to describe the look on the woman's face. I'd never been so glad that my hair was back to its natural color.

"I am Tansy Roberts," the woman announced, as if she was telling us she was a rock star or something. "I am Sarah's aunt."

This was, in other words, Aunt Tansy from Greenwich.

"Pleased to meet you," said Aunt Ruthie, and stuck out her hand. There was a beat and then The Greenwich Aunt shook The Bronx Aunt's hand.

"May I inquire why you wish to see my niece?" asked Aunt Tansy.

"You may. We have news as to the where-abouts of one Mitchell Redfern."

Aunt Tansy's pink mouth opened in surprise and her cheeks colored up like two red tulips. "Please sit down," she said and walked over to a long gold rope, which she pulled. I knew this was ringing a bell somewhere else in the house 'cause I'd seen it in the movies. The Aunt from Greenwich went on. "Is he..."

"He's okay," I said.

She looked at me as if to say, What do you know? because The Aunt from the Bronx had forgotten to introduce me and Elissa. Realizing this error, introductions were made.

"Where *is* Mitchell?" asked Aunt Tansy.

"He lives on Perry Street in the Village."

"What village?"

Me and Elissa looked at each other. "Greenwich Village," I said.

"Oh, dear," she said in a shocked tone.

Just then Baldy came in. "Madam, you rang?"

"Yes, Enfield, please ask Sarah to join us."

Tansy and Enfield! Where did they get these monikers? Aunt Tansy turned back to me. "How is Mitchell's health?"

"He's in a wheelchair now."

"I see." She shook her head sadly.

"Sarah lives with you alone?" asked Elissa.

I thought this was a little too nosy but I was glad she had the nerve to ask.

"Yes. Sarah's parents...well, when Sarah announced she was still going to marry Mitchell after his disease was diagnosed, her parents were horrified. They told her if she did they'd have nothing to do with her." Tansy smiled like she was proud of something. "But Sarah, I'm happy to say, is her own person."

"She said to her parents she'd marry him anyway?" asked The Aunt from the Bronx.

"Exactly. To be precise, she told them to go to hell." Aunt Tansy broke into a grin so sunny it felt like little beams of warm light had touched each one of us.

"Good for her," said Aunt Ruthie. "You have no objections to such a union?"

"I'm not a fool, Mrs. . . ."

"Call me Ruth, please."

"And please call me Tansy."

I watched Aunt Ruthie swallow and knew saying such a name wouldn't be real easy for her but she'd try.

"At any rate, Ruth, I'm not a fool and I know a life married to a man with an incurable disease would be problematic, but I also know love comes first. As young as Sarah is, she loves Mitchell deeply and is prepared to take what comes. I'm sorry to say Mitchell wasn't as brave. I'm sure, however, it wasn't because he didn't love her that he ran away."

"He loves her," I heard myself saying. "He didn't want to be dependent on her and be a burden."

"Yes, I can understand why he might feel that way, but . . ."

Sarah came into the room. I gotta admit she

was even prettier than her picture. They sure would make a good-looking couple. Feh!

Aunt Tansy filled her in and Sarah burst into tears. I think it was happiness that turned on the waterworks. When she got it under control she dabbed her baby blues with a tissue, came over to me, and kissed me on the cheek.

"Oh, thank you for coming here," she said.

It seemed like this kissing thing was getting out of hand. Famine or feast, like they say! But don't get me wrong . . . no complaints!

"Do you think he wants to see me?" asked Sarah.

"Well, to tell the truth, he probably doesn't. What I mean is I think he does but he doesn't know it. He keeps your picture by his bed."

Sarah blushed. "I keep his by mine," she said.

"Sarah, dear," said The Greenwich Aunt, "I think you should know that Mitchell's in a wheelchair. He is, after all, one of the unlucky people with multiple sclerosis."

Sarah looked very serious, but said nothing.

Then The Bronx Aunt spoke up. "You'll excuse me if I butt in here for a minute, Sarah. I just wish to say that if a person decided that a person did not want to spend her life with a person in a wheelchair, who might even get worse, that person would not be a bad person."

This, I confess, shocked me. And I guess it showed because Aunt Ruthie patted my hand and went on. "The thing is, there's no use kidding around. Marrying Mitchell means an unusual life, to say the least. A lot of sacrifice will be ahead."

"I know," said Sarah. "I've had a lot of time

to think about all this and I know it's why Mitch ran away. He didn't want me to be in that position. But it wasn't fair of him at all."

Me, I thought it was sort of a noble gesture but then Sarah made me see how it wasn't.

"Mitch gave me no credit for knowing my own mind and heart. I fell in love with his soul, his mind, his sweetness. It's true that when I first saw him he was running down a football field for a touchdown but it wasn't those fast-moving legs that I fell for."

So he'd been an athlete. He'd never ever let that one slip.

"It was cruel for Mitch to run away," Sarah went on. "You can't possibly know what his family and I have been through. Aunt Tansy too. We've had private detectives looking for him and everything. I'd just about given up hope of ever finding him. Will you take me to him?" she asked.

"Natch," I said. "That's why we've come."

"Now?"

I hadn't expected that. I don't know what I'd thought was going to happen, but her question caught me off guard. If I'd really thought about it I would've realized she'd want to see him as soon as possible. I looked at The Aunt from the Bronx and then at Elissa. Each one of them could've answered Sarah but they knew it was up to me. "Yeah, sure. Can't think of a better time." Except maybe in a hundred years, I thought.

"I'll just go give the Redferns a call and tell them Mitch has been found." She hurried out of the room while we cooled our heels.

And speaking of heels, I had a minute then

when I wished I could've been one. It's funny how sometimes when you do the right thing and know it, you wish maybe you were more of a rat. The rat gets the cheese, like they say, and right about now I felt like Billie was getting zip.

Then Aunt Tansy said, "We'll always be grateful to you, Billie, no matter how things turn out."

"What d'ya mean?" It seemed clear to me how things would work out.

"He may stick to his guns and refuse to come home with Sarah."

That had never dawned on me and for a second I felt happy and then I *did* feel like a rat. What *I* wanted or didn't want had nothing to do with it. What was important was what was best for Mitch.

"However," said The Greenwich Aunt, "at least we'll know he's alive."

Sarah was back. "His parents are so happy. They agreed I should see him first. Can we go now?"

We all made our way to the front door, where the two aunts shook hands and then, like on a signal, they hugged each other. Funny how people could look and seem so different but really be the same. Two Aunts In A Pod!

While we were riding back to New York the sun came out. Sarah and I were in the backseat and all the way home she never stopped asking me questions about Mitch. A kind of agony is what I felt.

Back in the Village we found a parking space on Charles Street a block away from Mitch's apartment. The plan was, I'd call him from a phone booth and see if he'd let me come over.

When I got there I'd explain what we'd done and tell him Sarah was just outside. If he said he didn't want to see me I'd tell him about Sarah on the phone, and if he said he didn't want to see *her*, Aunt Ruthie was prepared to break down the door.

I dialed his number. I rang eight times before he answered.

"It's Billie."

"Oh, Billie," he said, "thank God you called. I've missed you like crazy."

Seventeen

When I hung up the phone I stood in the booth thinking. There were a few things I could do. A, I could go back to the others and say there was no answer but that would only put the whole thing off; B, I could say someone else answered and told me Mitch had moved and nobody knew where to; C, I could just disappear. But that stank 'cause both Aunt Ruthie and Elissa knew where Mitch lived. There was, of course, D, which was to go ahead with the original plan. I felt depressed.

Mitch had missed me and was welcoming me back. I could be his, he could be mine, sort of, and now I had Sarah stashed in a car. I could've kicked myself for butting in the way I had. And then I remembered Sarah's face when she'd heard Mitch was alive and safe. The truth was, I had no choice. The ball, like they say, was in my court.

As slowly as I could I walked back to where the three of them waited. Then Sarah and I went to Mitch's apartment. She stayed in the hall while I went in.

He was sitting in his regular chair looking

more gorgeous than ever, a smile lighting up his face, crinkles around those big brown eyes, and my heart did a somersault the likes of which belonged only in the Olympics.

"Billie," he said, "I'm so glad to see you. Boy, have I been lonely without you."

It crossed my mind then that the guy missed me as a friend. I couldn't think there was anything romantic about it or I'd let poor Sarah stand in the hall forever.

"I missed you too, Mitch."

"Sit down. You look great."

"Yeah, thanks. You too." It hadn't even been a week since we'd seen each other.

"What've you been up to?"

That, I believe, is what is known as a big fat OPENING! To take it or not to take it, that was the question. The thing was, I hadn't really rehearsed. It was one thing to bring Sarah here and another to tell him. So I heard myself saying, "Not much."

"Billie, I want to apologize for the other day. I mean, asking you to leave. I want you to take back the keys and . . ."

"Mitch," I broke in 'cause I couldn't stand it another sec, "I've done something you might be mad about so before you offer me the keys I think, well, like you . . ."

He waved his hand, as if to say no matter what I'd done it didn't matter. "I still want you to know how sorry I am. I know you said those things because you like me and want to help and I think you're right."

"You do?"

He nodded. "I called you today but there was no answer." He reached down into the side of the chair and pulled out a small wrapped package. I could tell from the shape it was a book. "I bought you a present."

It wasn't the idea of him buying me a present that knocked me out so much but *how*. Then I thought I knew. "Mickey get it for you?"

"No. I went out."

"Oh, Mitch," I said, my eyes getting all teary. I got up and took the present from him.

"It's a book I like a lot," he said.

I unwrapped it. It was a book called *The Snow Goose* by Paul Gallico, and inside Mitch had written, "To my very special friend, Billie, who knows how to tell the truth. All my love, Mitch." I don't know if it was what he'd written or that he'd actually gone outside in his wheelchair or really knowing we were friends, or maybe all of it, but I couldn't stop the tears from going over the top. "Thank you," I said. "And thanks for all your truth too. About my hair and the talent thing. You were right."

"I guess we're even then. Now, what was it you wanted to tell me?"

Sarah! I'd forgotten all about her out there in the hall. Well, now we'd see if I'd blown it all or the guy really meant we were friends. "Mitch, I don't know how to tell you this and I hope you won't be mad, but if you are I guess you are. Here goes. Sarah's out in the hall."

I guess you could say he looked more confused than surprised. Associating me with Sarah was not right in the front of his brain. So I said, "Sarah Roberts," and swallowed hard.

"Sarah Roberts?"

"Yeah. She loves you, Mitch."

"Ah, Billie," he said and shook his head, sad

like. Then he asked me how I'd found her and I told him. "Another talent," he said. "She's out in the hall?"

I nodded. "Can I get her?"

He didn't answer.

"Mitch, you said I know how to tell the truth so here's some more. Sarah Roberts is no wimp. She's had a lot of time to think this whole thing over and she knows it's not gonna be a picnic to be with you."

"But Billie . . ."

"Save it and just listen. Sarah loves you. And it's not 'cause she pities you, like you're pathetic or something. The thing is, Mitch, you can't decide everything for everybody else. They have to decide for themselves. Like me. In the end I had to decide what to do about my hair. You couldn't decide for me what to do, any more than I can make the decision for you to see Sarah or you can decide that Sarah should be with somebody else. You get it, dumbbell?"

He actually laughed. "I think maybe I do. Why don't you tell her to come in?"

"Right." Just before I got to the door he called my name. "Yeah?"

"How do I look?" he goes.

"Beautiful," I said. And then I went out into the hall. She was looking all scared and pale. "It's okay."

"He wants to see me?"

"Yeah. He's nervous though."

"Well," Sarah said, "that makes two of us."

"You'd better go in."

"You're not coming?"

"I think I'd be a third wheel."

She smiled and nodded. "I don't know how to thank you."

"You already did. You got my phone number?"

"Yes. I'll call you later. Well," she said, patting her hair into place, "here goes."

In a second she was gone. Inside. And I was outside. My good deed was done and I felt rotten. I was sure they'd work it out, so I should've been happy. Sarah had Mitch and Mitch had Sarah. And come to think of it, Elissa had Mickey and The Mother had The Painter and Aunt Ruthie had Marvin and I had Zip.

Fifteen minutes later The Aunt and Elissa and I were sipping cappuccinos in Vinnie's. I'd filled them in on what had happened and then I said how lousy I felt.

"This is a shock to my ears," said Aunt Ruthie. She popped a piece of apple pie into her shocked mouth.

"Why should I feel happy? Everybody's got somebody but me."

"You have yourself," she said. "And what a self it is."

"I think you're pretty neat," goes Elissa. "You could've kept Mitch hidden away for yourself."

"But he never loved me like that." It wasn't too easy to say right out loud but I guess it made it real.

"Listen, tzotzkalla, you gave two people a chance . . . you gave them back their lives."

I felt rotten saying this but I said it anyway: "And what did I get?"

Aunt Ruthie from the Bronx took a sip of cap, licked her lips, and focused her peepers on me. "In my life I have come to see that we do not always know right away what we get out of being a decent human being. And there is not, I have discovered, always a payoff. Sometimes we do things because we know it's right and that's all there is to it. More than this I cannot tell you."

And then I remembered my prayer. I had asked to have things work out the way they should. Someone once said you should be careful what you pray for. I guess when I said that prayer I had a different ending in mind. But whether I liked the ending or not, this is the way it was.

We walked The Aunt to her car.

"Aunt Ruthie, I don't know what we'd do without you," from Elissa.

"You'd live," she goes. "And Billie, I want you to remember this: There are plenty of fish in the sea."

"Hey, you got it right," I said.

"That just shows," she said, "anything is possible!"

There were kisses and thanks and then The Aunt was gone. Me and Elissa started walking, no place special in mind. Since it was late on a Saturday afternoon, a lot of freaky-looking people were wandering around SoHo. Funny how I saw it all differently now. I actually felt sorry for the ones with pink and green and blue hair. I mean it's okay to do it, to express yourself any way you want, but I think I knew why they needed to do it in that particular way and it made me sad. I also knew I'd never have to get attention like that again.

On Spring Street near Sullivan there were a couple of park benches, and we sat down and watched the passing parade. After a while Elissa goes, "Dino's getting home on Monday."

"So?"

She shrugged. "Maybe he'll be different."

"Maybe." I hoped he would be, but in terms of me and him I didn't think it would make much difference and told Elissa so.

"Do you think Mitch'll go back to Greenwich with Sarah?" she asked.

"I hope so." And I did, I really deep-down did. When you know something's right, you know it. "In fact, I'm sure of it."

"What d'ya think is gonna happen to him? I mean with his disease?"

"I dunno. He could go on just like he is now for a long, long time. The main thing is," I said, "he won't be running away from everything anymore. There's no place to run when you face up to stuff. Like me."

"You?"

"Yeah, me. There was a whole lot of stuff I knew while it was going on but I pretended I didn't know and that got me nowhere. Dino, for instance."

"How so?"

"Elissa, I always knew it was no good. From day one I knew but I made like it was so I wouldn't be alone. You had a boyfriend so I thought I should have one. That's nuts."

"Guess that's no reason to have a boyfriend," she said.

"Right. And somewhere, deep in my heart, I knew how Mitch *really* felt about me all along."

"You did?" she said, acting real surprised.

I gave her one of my best who-you-kidding looks. "And *you* didn't?"

Sheepish is how she looked. Then I said, "Listen, it's not your fault, if you'd wanted me to pretend about something I would've. Notice I said *would've*. No more. I've even been pretending that The Father and The Mother were gonna get it together again."

"You never told me."

"Too crazy to say out loud. But the truth is The Father is a big loser and that hurts."

"And my mother's never gonna get better, is she?"

My pal looked so sad, I gave her hand a squeeze. "The thing is you have to look stuff in the eye for what it is *now*. Like, *now* The Father is a two-year-old and *now* Sylvia is not eating and acting crazy, and *now* Mitch is with Sarah. See what I mean?"

Elissa said, "It's easier the other way. Pretending."

"You wanna know something? It really isn't. All it does is put the hurt off for a while."

"I guess."

"And *you* know what else?" I said.

"What?"

"None of it, the truth that is, kills you, no matter how awful it is 'cause here we are."

"I think you're right."

"For once in my life, I think I am. Let's go."

We walked up Sullivan holding hands and saying nothing. We were just enjoying being pals. At the corner we hugged, then went our separate ways, promising to meet the next day like always.

I started across Prince Street to my loft. I remembered then that I was supposed to have dinner with The Mother and The Painter. An actual invitation had been extended. Pretty soon, I figured, it would be an everyday occurrence, 'cause it sure looked like it was getting serious.

If this had been a movie, just as I opened the front door of my building a handsome guy would be coming out and we'd bump into each other and then we'd fall in love.

But it wasn't a movie and no one was coming out. Except Roger, my upstairs neighbor.

"Hiya, squirt," he said.

This was reality. I walked down the hall and rang for the elevator. So I didn't feel one hundred million percent okay. Why should I? On the other hand I didn't feel one hundred million percent lousy. Some days are up and some are down and sometimes things go your way and sometimes they don't. And sometimes it's just Feh!

I think they call it Life and it's okay with me.

ABOUT THE AUTHOR

SANDRA SCOPPETTONE is the author of three previous young adult novels. They are *Trying Hard to Hear You*, *The Late Great Me*, and *Happy Endings Are All Alike*. She also writes novels for adults. Ms. Scoppettone lives in New York City and Greenport, New York.